© JUDY KING RIENIETS 81

MADWAND

ROGER ZELAZNY

SF
ace books
A Division of Charter Communications Inc.
A GROSSET & DUNLAP COMPANY
51 Madison Avenue
New York, New York 10010

This one is for Trent.

I.

I am not certain.

It sometimes seems as if I have always been here, yet I know that there must have been a time before my advent.

And sometimes it seems as if I have only just lately arrived. From where I might have come, I have no idea. Recently, I have found this vaguely troubling, but only recently.

For a long while, I drifted through these halls, across the battlements, up and down the towers, expanding or contracting as I chose, to fill a room—or a dozen—or to snake my way through the homes of mice, to trace the sparkling cables of the spider's web. Nothing moves in this place but that I am aware of it.

Yet I was not fully aware of myself until recently, and the acts I have just recited have the dust of dreams strewn over them, myself the partial self of the dreamer. Yet—.

Yet I do not sleep. I do not dream. However, I seem now to know of many things which I have never experienced.

Perhaps it is that I am a slow learner, or perhaps something has recently stimulated my awareness to the point where all the echoes of thoughts have brought about something new within me—a sense of self which I did not formerly possess, a knowledge of separateness, of my apartness from those things which are not-me.

If this is the case, I would like to believe that it has to do with my reason for being. I have also recently begun feeling that I should have a reason for being, that it is important that I have a reason for being. I have no idea, however, as to what this could be.

It has been said—again, recently—that this place is haunted. But a ghost, as I understand it, is some non-physical survival of someone or something which once existed in a more solid form. I have never encountered such an entity in my travels through this place, though lately it has occurred to me that the reference could be to me in my more tangible moments. Still, I do not believe that I am a ghost, for I have no recollection of the requisite previous state.

Of course, it is difficult to be certain in a matter such as this, for I lack knowledge concerning whatever laws might govern such situations.

And this is another area of existence of which I have but recently become aware: laws—restrictions, compulsions, areas of freedom . . . They seem to be everywhere, from the dance of the tiniest particles to the turning of the world, which may be the reason I had paid them such small heed before. That which is ubiquitous is almost unnoticed. It is so easy to flow in accordance with the usual without reflecting upon it. It may well be that it was the occurrence of the unusual which served to rouse this faculty within me, and along with it the realization of my own existence.

Then, too, in accordance with the laws with which I have become aware, I have observed a phenomenon which I refer to as the persistence of pattern. The two men who sit talking within the room where I hover like a slowly turning, totally transparent cloud an arm's distance out from the highest bookshelf nearest the window—these two men are both patterned upon similar lines of symmetry, though I become aware of many differences within these limits, and the wave disturbances which they cause within the air when communicating with one another are also patterned things possessing, or possessed by, rules of their own. And if I attend very closely, I can even become aware of their thoughts behind, and sometimes even before, these disturbances. These, too, seem to be patterned, but at a much higher level of complexity.

It would seem to follow that if I were a ghost something of my previous pattern might have persisted. But I am without particular form, capable of great expansions and contractions, able to permeate anything I have so far encountered. And there is no special resting state to which I feel constrained to return.

Along with my nascent sense of identity and my ignorance as to what it is that I am, I do feel something else: a certainty that I am incomplete. There is a thing lacking within me, which, if I were to discover it, might well provide me with that reason for being which I so desire. There are times when I feel as if I had been, in a way, sleeping for a long while and but recently been awakened by the commotions in this place—awakened to find myself robbed of some essential instruction. (I have only lately learned the concept "robbed" because one of the men I now regard is a thief.)

If I am to acquire a completeness, it would seem that I must pursue it myself. I suppose that, for now, I ought to make this pursuit my reason for being. Yes. Self-knowledge, the quest after identity . . . These would seem a good starting place. I wonder whether anyone else has ever had such a problem? I will pay close attention to what the men are saying.

I do not like being uncertain.

Pol Detson had arranged the seven figurines into a row on the desk before him. A young man, despite the white streak through his hair, he leaned forward and extended a hand in their direction. For a time he moved it slowly, passing his fingertips about the entire group, then in and out, encircling each gem-studded individual. Finally, he sighed and withdrew. He crossed the room to where the small, black-garbed man sat, left leg crooked over the arm of his chair, a wineglass in either hand, the contents of both aswirl. He accepted one from him and raised it to his lips.

"Well?" the smaller man, Mouseglove by name, the thief, asked him when he lowered it.

Pol shook his head, moved a chair so that his field of vision took in both Mouseglove and the statuettes, seated himself.

"Peculiar," he said at last. "Almost everything tosses off a thread, something to give you a hold over it, even if you have to fight for it, even if it only does it occasionally."

"Perhaps this is not the proper occasion."

Pol leaned forward, set his glass upon the desk. He flexed his fingers before him and placed their tips together. He began rubbing them against one another with small, circular movements. After perhaps half a minute, he drew them apart and reached toward the desk.

He chose the nearest figure—thin, female, crowned with a red stone, hands clasped beneath the breasts—and began making a wrapping motion about it, though Mouseglove could detect no substance to be engaged in the process. Finally, his fingers moved as if he were tying a series of knots in a nonexistent string. Then he moved away, seating himself again, drawing his hands slowly after him as if playing out a line with some tension on it.

He sat unmoving for a long while. Then the figure on the desk jerked slightly and he lowered his hands.

"No good," he said, rubbing his eyes and reaching to recover his wineglass. "I can't seem to get a handle on it. They are not like anything else I know about."

"They're special, all right," Mouseglove observed, "considering the dance they put me through. And from the glimpses they gave

you at Anvil Mountain, I have the feeling they could talk to you
right now—if they wanted to."

"Yes. They were helpful enough—in a way—at the time. I wonder why they won't communicate now?"

"Perhaps they have nothing to say."

I found myself puzzled by the manner in which these men
spoke of those seven small statues on the desk, as if they were
alive. I drew nearer and examined them. I had noted lines of force
going from the man Pol's fingertips to them, shortly after he had
spoken of "threads" and performed his manipulations. I had also
detected a throbbing of power in the vicinity of his right forearm,
where he bore the strangely troubling mark of the dragon—a thing
about which I feel I should know more than I do—but I had seen
no threads. Nor had I noted any sort of reaction from the figures,
save for the small jerking movement of the one as the shell of
force was repelled.

I settled down about them, contracting, feeling the textures of the
various materials of which they had been formed. Cold, lifeless. It
was only the words of the men which laid any mystery upon them.

Continuing this commerce of surfaces, I grew even smaller, concentrating my attention now upon that figure which Pol had momentarily bound. My action then was as prompt as my decision: I
began to pour myself into it, flowing through the minuscule openings—

The burn! It was indescribable, the searing feeling that passed
through my being. Expanding, filling the room, passing beyond it
into the night, I knew that it must be that thing referred to as pain.
I had never experienced it before and I wanted never to feel it
again.

I continued to seek greater tenuosity, for in it lay a measure of
alleviation.

Pol had been correct concerning the figure. It was, somehow,
alive. It did not wish to be disturbed.

Beyond the walls of Rondoval, the pain began to ease. I felt a
stirring within me . . . something which had always been there
but was just now beginning to creep into awareness . . .

"What was that?" Pol said. "It sounded like a scream, but—"

"I didn't hear anything," Mouseglove answered, straightening.
"But I just felt a jolt—as if I'd been touched by someone who'd
walked across a heavy rug, only stronger, longer . . . I don't

know. It gave me a chill. Maybe you stirred something up, playing with that statue."

"Maybe," Pol said. "For a moment, it felt as if there were something peculiar right here in the room with us."

"There must be a lot of unusual things about this old place— with both of your parents having been practicing sorcerers. Not to mention your grandparents, and theirs."

Pol nodded and sipped his wine.

"There are times when I feel acutely aware of my lack of formal training in the area."

He raised his right hand slightly above shoulder-level, extended his index finger and moved it rapidly through a series of small circles. A book bound in skin of an indeterminate origin appeared suddenly in his hand, a gray and white feather bookmark protruding from it.

"My father's diary," he announced, lowering the volume and opening it to the feather. "Now here," he said, running his finger down the righthand page, pausing and staring, "he tells how he defeated and destroyed an enemy sorcerer, capturing his spirit in the form of one of the figures. Elsewhere, he talks of some of the others. But all that he says at the end here is, 'It will prove useful in the task to come. If six will not do to force the wards I shall have seven, or even eight.' Obviously, he had something very specific in mind. Unfortunately, he did not commit it to paper."

"Further along perhaps?"

"I'll be up late again reading. I've taken my time with it these past months because it is not a pleasant document. He wasn't a very nice guy."

"I know that. It is good that you learn it from his own words, though."

"His words about forcing the wards—Do they mean anything at all to you?"

"Not a thing."

"A good sorcerer would find some way to learn it from the materials at hand, I'm sure."

"I'm not. Those things seem extremely potent. As for your own abilities, you seem to have come pretty far without training. I'd give a lot to be able to pull that book trick—with, say, someone's jewelry. Where'd you get it from, anyway?"

Pol smiled.

"I didn't want to leave it lying around, so I bound it with a golden strand and ordered it to retreat into one of those placeless places between the worlds, as I saw them arrayed on my journey here. It vanished then, but whenever I wish to continue reading it I merely draw upon the thread and summon it."

"Gods! You could do that with a suit of armor, a rack of weapons, a year's supply of food, your entire library, for that matter! You can make yourself invincible!"

Pol shook his head.

"Afraid not," he said. "The book and the jumble-box are all I've been keeping there, because I wouldn't want either to fall into anyone else's hands. If I were traveling, I could add my guitar. Much more, though, and it would become too great a burden. Their mass somehow gets added to my own. It's as if I'm carrying around whatever I send through."

"So that's where the box has gotten to. I remember your locating it, that day we went back to Anvil Mountain . . ."

"Yes. I almost wish I hadn't."

"You couldn't really hope to recover his body or your scepter from that crater."

"No, that's not what I meant. It was just seeing all that—waste—that bothered me. I—"

He slammed his fist against the arm of his chair.

"Damn those statues! It sometimes seems they were behind it all! If I could just get them to—Hell!"

He drained his glass and went to refill it.

The sensation ebbed. I did not like that experience. The room and its inhabitants were now tiny within the cloud of myself, and more uncertainties were now present: I did not know what it was that had caused me pain, nor how it produced that effect. I felt that I should learn these things, so as to avoid it in the future. I did not know how to proceed.

I also felt that it might be useful for me to learn how to produce this effect in others, so that I could cause them to leave me alone. How might I do this? If there were a means of contact it would seem that it could go either way, once the technique were mastered . . .

Again, the stirring of memory. But I was distracted. Someone approached the castle. It was a solitary human of male gender. I was aware of the distinction because of my familiarity with the girl Nora who had dwelled within for a time before returning to her own people. This man wore a brown cloak and dark clothing. He came drifting out of the northwest, mounted upon one of the lesser kin of the dragons who dwell below. His hair was yellow, and in places white. He wore a short blade. He circled. He could not miss the sign of the one lighted room. He began to descend, silent as a leaf or an ash across the air. I believed that he would land at the far end of the courtyard, out of sight of the library window.

Yes.

Within the room the men were talking, about the battle at the place called Anvil Mountain, where Pol destroyed his stepbrother, Mark Marakson. Pol, I gather, is a sorcerer and Mark was something else, similar but opposite. A sorcerer is one who manipulates forces as I saw Pol do with the statue, and the book. Now, dimly, I recalled another sorcerer. His name was Det.

". . . You've been brooding over those figures too long," Mouseglove was saying. "If there were an easy answer, you'd have found it by now."

"I know," Pol replied. "That's why I'm looking for something more complicated."

"I don't have any special knowledge of magic," Mouseglove said, "but it looks to me as if the problem does not lie completely in that area."

"What do you mean?"

"Facts, man. You haven't enough plain, old-fashioned information to be sure what you're up against here, what it is that you should be doing. You've had a couple of months to ransack this library, to play every magical game you can think of with the stiff dolls. If the answer were to be found that way, you'd have turned it up. It's just not here. You are going to have to look somewhere else."

"Where?" Pol asked.

"If I knew that, I'd have told you before now. I've been away from the world I knew for over twenty years. It must have changed a bit in that time. So I'm hardly one to be giving directions. But you know I'd only intended to remain here until I'd recovered from my injury. I've been feeling fine for some time now. I've been loath to leave, though, because of you. I don't like seeing you drive yourself against a crazy mystery day after day. There are enough half-mad wizards in the world, and I think that's where you may be heading—not to mention the possibility of your setting off something which may simply destroy you on the spot. I think you ought to get out, get away from the problem for a time. You'd said you wanted to see more of this world. Do it now. Come with me—tomorrow. Who knows? You may even come across some of the information you seek in your travels."

"I don't know . . ." Pol began. "I do want to go, but—Tomorrow?"

"Tomorrow."

"Where would we be heading?"

"Over to the coast, I was thinking, and then north along it. You can pick up a lot of news in port cities—"

Pol raised his hand and cocked his head. Mouseglove nodded and rose to his feet.

"Your warning system still working?" Mouseglove whispered.

Pol nodded and turned toward the door.

"Then it can't be any—"

The sound came again, and with it the form of a light-haired man appeared in the doorway, smiling.

"Good evening, Pol Detson," he stated, raising his left hand and jerking it through a series of quick movements, "and goodbye."

Pol fell to his knees, his face suddenly bright red. Mouseglove rounded the desk. Picking up one of the statuettes and raising it like a club, he moved toward the brown-cloaked stranger.

The man made a sudden movement with his right hand and the thief was halted, spun and slammed back against the wall to his left. The figurine fell from his grip as he slumped to the floor.

As this occurred, Pol raised his hands beside his cheeks and then gestured outward. His face began returning to its normal color as he climbed to his feet.

"I might ask 'Why?' " he said, his own hands moving now, rotating in opposite directions.

The stranger continued to smile and made a sweeping movement with one hand, as if brushing away an insect.

"And I might answer you," said the other, "but it would take some coercion."

"Very well," said Pol. "I'm willing."

He felt his dragonmark throb and the air was alive with strands. Reaching out, he seized a fistful, shook them and snapped them like a lash toward the other's face.

The man reached out and caught them as they arrived. A numbing shock traveled up Pol's arm and it fell limply to his side. The density of the strands between them increased to a level he had never before witnessed, partly obscuring his view of his opponent.

Pol made a large sweeping motion with his left hand, gathering in a ball of them. Immediately, he willed it to fire and cast the blazing orb toward the other.

The man deflected it with the back of his right hand and then flung both arms upward and outward.

The light in the room began to throb. The air became so filled with the lines of power that they seemed to merge, becoming huge, swimming, varicolored patterns obscuring much of the prospect, including the stranger.

As the pulse in his dragonmark overcame the numbness in his right arm, Pol sent his will through it, seeking a clearer image of his adversary. Immediately, the form of the other man began to glow, as the rainbow-work wove itself to closure. The room disappeared, and Pol became aware that his form, too, had become luminescent.

The two of them faced one another across a private universe built entirely of moving colors.

Pol saw the man raise his hands, cupping them before him. Immediately, a green serpent raised its head from within them and slithered forth, moving in Pol's direction.

Pol could feel a raw creation force moving all about him. He reached out and up, beginning a rapid series of shaping movements. A huge, gray bird came into being between his hands. He laid his will upon it and released it. It flashed forward and dove upon the snake, catching at it with its talons, striking with its beak. The serpent twisted its body and struck at the bird, missing.

Looking past this contest, Pol saw that the man was now juggling a number of balls of colored light. Even as the bird rose, bearing the struggling snake in its talons, to flap upward and merge with the kaleidoscopic field which surrounded them, Pol saw the man cast the first blazing ball in his direction.

Smiling, Pol shaped a tennis racquet and saw a look of puzzlement cross his adversary's features as he regarded the unfamiliar instrument.

He slammed the first ball back at the man just as the second was released. The sorcerer dropped the remaining balls and dove to the side to avoid the return. Pol batted the second one out-of-court as the man rolled forward and came to his feet, his right hand snapping outward, something long and black moving with it.

He swung the racquet and missed as the whip caught him about the neck and jerked him forward. He felt himself falling. Dropping the racquet, he reached for the choking thing that held him, to seize it, unwind it—

It jerked again and the world began to spin and darken. It continued to tighten, and he heard the sound of laughter, coming nearer . . .

"Not much of a contest," he heard the other say.

Then there was an explosion and everything went black.

It was instructive to observe the exchange of forces between Pol and the visitor. Also, mildly unsettling, as it occurred to me that they might be inducing pain in one another. Yet, they had wanted to do it or they wouldn't have. I was more interested in the manipulations than I was in their progressive wearing down of one another, because I felt that I might be able to engage in that sort of activity myself and I wished to be further informed. Its abrupt ending came as a surprise to me. Save for small, less complex creatures, I had not seen one being end another's existence. Indeed, it had not occurred to me that these larger ones could be ended. I felt as if I should have taken a part in it, though on which side and in which direction, I could not say. I was also uncertain as to why I felt this way.

Where there had been three there were now two. I did not understand why they had done it, nor how the lance of force had come from the statuette to terminate the stranger before Mouseglove's projectile reached his head.

Pol shook his head. His neck was sore. He rubbed it and opened his eyes. He was lying on the floor beside the desk. Slowly, he pushed himself into a seated position.

The stranger lay upon his back near the door, right arm outflung, left across his breast. A piece of his forehead was missing and his right eye was a crimson pool.

To his left, leaning against a bookshelf, Mouseglove stood rubbing his eyes. His right arm hung at his side and in his hand was the pistol he had carried away from Anvil Mountain. When he saw Pol move he dropped his left hand and smiled weakly.

"Are you all right?" he asked.

"I guess so. Except for a stiff neck. What about yourself?"

"I don't know what he hit me with. It affected my sight for a while. When I came around, the two of you seemed to be pulsing

into and out of existence. I wasn't able to get a shot at him till the
last time he came through." He replaced the weapon in a holster
behind his belt and moved forward, extending his hand. "Everything seems normal enough now."

Pol accepted his hand and rose. They both crossed the room
and looked down at the dead man. Mouseglove immediately knelt
and began searching him. After several minutes, he shook his
head, unfastened the brown cloak and covered the man with it.

"Nothing," he said, "to tell who he is or why he came. I take it
you have no idea?"

"None."

They returned to their seats and the wine flask, Mouseglove restoring the fallen figurine on the way.

"Either he had some reason for disliking you and came by to do
something about it," Mouseglove said, "or somebody else who
feels that way sent him. In the first case, some friend of his might
come along later to continue the work. In the second, another may
be sent as soon as it is known that this one failed. Either way, it
would appear that more trouble will be forthcoming."

Pol nodded. He rose and removed a book from a shelf high on
the lefthand wall. He returned to his seat and began paging
through it.

"This one got through all of your alarm spells without giving
warning," Mouseglove continued.

"He was better than I am," Pol said, without looking up from
the book.

"So what is to be done?"

"Here," Pol said, locating the page he sought and reading
silently for a time. "I had been wondering about this for some
time," he went on. "Every four years there is a gathering of sorcerers at Belken, a mountain to the northwest. Ever hear of it?"

"Of course—as a good thing to stay away from."

"It will begin in about two weeks. I've decided to attend."

"If they're all like this fellow—" Mouseglove nodded toward the
form upon the floor. "—I don't think it would be a very good
idea."

Pol shook his head.

"The description makes it sound rather peaceful. Advanced
practitioners discuss theory with one another, apprentices are initiated, rites involving more than one sorcerer get tried out, exotic
articles are traded and sold, new effects demonstrated. . ."

"The person behind this attempt on your life may be there."

"Exactly. I'd like to settle this quickly. It may all be some sort of misunderstanding. After all, I haven't been around long enough to have made any real enemies. And if the one I seek isn't there, I may learn something about him—if there is such a person. Either way, it makes it seem worthwhile."

"And that will be your only reason for going?"

"Well, no. I also feel the need for some formal training in the Art. Perhaps I can pick up a few pointers at something like that."

"I don't know, Pol . . . It sounds kind of risky."

"Not going may prove even more dangerous in the long run."

They heard a scraping noise and a popping sound from the courtyard. Both rose and moved to the window. Looking downward, they saw nothing. Pol seemed to stroke the air with his fingertips.

"The man's mount," he said finally. "It's freed itself of whatever restraints he'd laid upon it and is preparing to depart." He moved his hand rapidly, raising the other one as well. "Maybe I can get a line on it, trace it back to where it came from."

The lesser kin of the dragon rose in the northeast and swept through a wide, rising arc, leftward.

"No good," Pol said, lowering his hands. "Missed him."

Mouseglove shrugged.

"I guess you won't be going with me," he said, "if you'll be heading for that convocation, in the other direction."

Pol nodded.

"I'll leave tomorrow, too, though. I'd rather be moving about than staying in one place between now and then. So we can take the trail for a little way together."

"You won't be riding Moonbird?"

"No, I want to see something of the countryside, too."

"Traveling alone also has its hazards."

"I'd imagine they are fewer for a sorcerer."

"Perhaps," Mouseglove replied.

The dark form of the dragonmount dwindled against the northern sky, vanished within a mountain's shadow.

II.

That night, as I permeated the dead man's body, seeking traces within his brain cells, I learned that his name had been Keth and that he had served one greater than himself. Nothing more. As I slid into and out of higher spaces, as I terminated a rat in a drainage channel in the manner I had recently learned, as I threaded my way among moonbeams in the old tower and slid along rafters in search of spiders, I thought upon the evening's doings and on all manner of existential questions which had not troubled me previously.

The energies of the creatures which I had taken had a bracing effect upon my overall being. I wandered through new areas of thought. Other beings existed in multitudes, yet I had never encountered another such as myself. Did this mean that I was unique? If not, where were the others? If so, why? From whence did I come? Was there a special reason for my existence? If yes, what could it be?

I swirled across the ramparts. I descended to the caverns far below and passed among the sleeping dragons and the other creatures. I felt no kinship with any of them.

It did not occur to me until much later that I must possess some particular attachment to Rondoval itself, else I might long ago have wandered off. I realized that I did prefer it and its environs to those other portions of the countryside into which I had ventured. Something had kept calling me back. What?

I returned to Pol's sleeping form and examined him very carefully, as I had every night since his arrival. And I found myself, as always, hovering above the dragonmark upon his right forearm. It, too, attracted me. For what reason, I could not say. It was at about the time of this man's arrival that I had begun the movement which had culminated in my present state of self-awareness. Was it somehow his doing? Or—the place having been deserted for as long as it had been—would the prolonged presence of anyone have worked the same effect within me?

My desire for purpose returned to me strongly. I began to feel that my apparent deficiency in this area might have been accidental, that perhaps I should possess a compulsion, that there was something I should be doing but had somehow lost or never learned. How significant, I wondered, was this feeling? Again, I was uncertain. But I began to understand what had produced my present attitude of inquiry.

Pol would be departing on the morrow. My memories of a time before his time had already become dim. Would I return to my more selfless state when he left? I did not believe so, yet I was willing to concede that he had played some part in my awakening into identity.

I realized at that moment that I was trying to make a decision. Should I remain at Rondoval or should I accompany Pol? And in either case, why?

I tried to terminate a bat in flight but it got away from me.

The two of them took the northern trail on foot that morning, traveling together through the pass and downward to the spring-touched green of the forest to the place of the crossroads Pol had marked upon the map he bore.

They rested their packs against the bole of a large oak, still darkly damp with the morning dew, and considered the mists which dwindled and faded even as they watched, while the sun became a bright bulge upon the slope of a mountain to their right. From somewhere behind them the first tentative notes of birdsong were commenced and then abandoned.

"You will be out of the hills by evening," said Pol, looking to the right. "It will be a few days before I get down, and then I'll have to climb again later. You'll be basking in the seabreeze while I'm still shivering my ass off. Well, good luck to you and thanks again—"

"Save the speech," said Mouseglove. "I'm coming along."

"To Belken?"

"All the way."

"Why?"

"I allowed myself to get too curious. Now I want to see how it all ends."

"It may well end indeed."

"You don't really believe that or you wouldn't be going. Come on! Don't try to talk me out of it. You might succeed."

Mouseglove raised his pack and moved off to the left. Shortly,

Pol joined him. The sun looked over the mountain's shoulder and
the gates of dawn were opened. Their shadows ran on before
them.

That night they camped within a stand of pine trees, and Pol
had a dream which felt like no dream he had ever known before.
There was a clarity and a quality of consciousness involved which
spun it past his inner eye with a disturbing simulation of reality,
while in all aspects it was invested with a foreboding air of menace
and yet possessed him with a certain dark joy.

Seven pale flames were moving in slow procession widdershins
about him, as if summoning him, spirit fashion, to appear in their
midst. He rose up slowly out of his body and stood like a blood-
less image of himself. At this, they halted and left the ground. He
followed them to treetop height and beyond. Then they escorted
him northward, moving higher and faster beneath a sky filled with
palely illuminated clouds. Grotesque shapes seemed to fill the
trees below, the mountains about him. The wind made a whining
sound and black forms flitted out of his way. The terrain rippled
in dark waves as his speed increased. The wind became a howling
thing, though he felt neither cold nor pressure from it.

At last, a huge, dark form loomed before him, set halfway up a
mountainside, dotted here and there with small illumination;
walled, turreted, heavy, high, it was a castle at least the size of
Rondoval and in better condition.

There followed a break in his dream-awareness from which he
recovered after an eon or a moment to a feeling of cold, of
dampness. He stood before a massive double-door, heavily ironbound and hung with huge rings. It was inscribed with the figure
of a serpent, spikes driven through it; the crucified form of a great
bird hung above it. Where it was located, he had no idea, but it
seemed suddenly familiar—as though he had glimpsed it repeatedly
in other dreams, forgotten until this instant. He swayed slightly
forward, realizing as he did that the chill he experienced hung
about the Gate itself like an invisible aura, increasing perceptibly
with each tiny movement he made toward it.

The flames burned silently, sourcelessly, at either hand. He was
overwhelmed with a desire to pass through the Gate, but he
had no idea as to how this might be accomplished. The doors
looked far too formidable to yield to the strength of any solitary
mortal . . .

He awoke cold and wondering, pulling his covering higher and

drawing it more tightly about him. The next morning he remembered the dream but did not speak of it. And that night it was partly repeated . . .

He stood again before the dusky Gate, with the recalled sensations but few specific images of his journey to the place. This time he stood with his arms upraised, pleading in ancient words for them to open before him. With a mighty creaking they obeyed, moving outward a short distance, releasing a small breeze and an icy chill along with tendrils of mist and a sound of distant wailing. He moved forward to enter . . .

On each night of that first week on the road, he returned to that dream and traveled further into it, losing his flamelike companions when he passed beyond the Gate. Alone, he drifted across a blasted landscape—gray and bronze, black and umber—beneath a dark, red-streaked sky where a barely illuminated, coppery orb hung still in what could be the west. It was a place of shadow and stone, sand and mist, of cold and wailing winds, sudden fires and slow, crawling things which refused to register themselves upon his memory. It was a place of sinister, sentient lights, dark caves and ruined statues of monstrous form and mien. Some small part of him seemed to regret that he took such pleasure in the prospect . . .

And the night that he saw the creatures—scaled, coarse monstrosities; long-armed, hulking parodies of the human form—sliding, hopping, lurching in pursuit of the lone man who fled before them across that landscape, he looked down with a certain anticipation.

The man ran between a pair of high stone pillars, cried out when he found himself in a rocky declivity having no other exit. The creatures entered and laid hold of him. They forced him to the ground and began tearing at him. They beat at him and flayed him, the ground growing even darker about them.

Abruptly, one of the creatures shrieked and drew back from the ghastly gathering. Its long, scaly right arm had been changed into something short and pale. The others uttered mocking noises and seized upon it. Holding the struggling creature, they returned their attention to the thing upon the ground. Bending forward, they wrenched and bit at it. It was no longer recognizable as anything human. But it was not unrecognizable.

It had altered under their moist invasions, becoming something larger, something resembling themselves in appearance, while the beast they held to witness had shrunken, growing softer and lighter and stranger.

Nor was it unrecognizable. It had become human in form, and whole.

Those who held the man pushed him and he fell. In the meantime, the demonic thing upon the ground was left alone as the others drew back from it. Its limbs twitched and it struggled to rise.

The man scrambled to his feet, stumbled, then raced forward, passing between the pillars, howling. Immediately, the dark creatures emitted sharp cries and, pushing and clawing against one another, moved to pursue the fleeing changeling, the one who had somehow been of a substance with him joining in.

Pol heard laughter and awoke to find it his own. It ended abruptly, and he lay for a long while staring at moonlit clouds through the dark branches of the trees.

They rode one day in the wagon of a farmer and his son and accompanied a pedlar for half a day. Beyond this—and encounters with a merchant and a physician headed in the opposite direction —they met no one taking the same route until the second week. Then, a sunny afternoon, they spied the dust and dark figures of a small troop before them in the distance.

It was late afternoon when they finally overtook the group of travelers. It consisted of an old sorcerer, Ibal Shenson, accompanied by his two apprentices, Nupf and Suhuy, and ten servants— four of whom were engaged in the transportation of the sedan chair in which Ibal rode.

It was to Nupf—a short, thin, mustachioed youth with long, dark hair—that Pol first addressed himself, since this one was walking at the rear of the retinue.

"Greetings," he said, and the man moved his right hand along an inconspicuous arc as he turned to face him.

As had been happening with increasing frequency when confronted with manifestations of the Art, Pol's second vision came reflexively into play. He saw a shimmering gray strand loop itself and move as if to settle over his head. With but the faintest throb of the dragonmark he raised his hand and brushed it aside.

"Here!" he said. "Is that the way to return the greeting of a fellow traveler?"

A look of apprehension widened the other's eyes, jerked at his mouth.

"My apologies," he said. "One never knows about travelers. I was merely acting to safeguard my master. I did not realize you were a brother in the Art."

"And now that you do . . . ?"

"You are headed for the meeting at Belken?"

"Yes."

"I will speak with my master, who no doubt will invite you to accompany us."

"Go ahead."

"Who shall I tell him sends greetings?"

"Pol Detson—and this is Mouseglove."

"Very well."

He turned and moved to catch up with the bearers. Pol and Mouseglove followed.

Looking over the apprentice's shoulder, Pol glimpsed the old sorcerer himself before the man addressed him. Swathed in blue garments, a gray shawl over his shoulders, a brown rug upon his lap, it was difficult to estimate his size, though he gave the impression of smallness and fragility. His nose was sharp, his eyes pale and close-set; his cheeks and forehead were deeply creased, the skin mottled; his hair was thick, long, very black and looked like a wig—for his beard was sparse and gray. His hands were out of sight beneath the rug.

"Come nearer," he hissed, turning his head toward Pol and squinting.

After he did so, Pol held his breath, becoming aware of the other's.

"Detson? Detson?" the man asked. "From where have you come?"

"Castle Rondoval," Pol replied.

"I thought the place deserted all these years. Who is lord there now?"

"I am."

There was a stirring beneath the brown coverlet. A big-jointed, dark-veined hand emerged. It moved slowly toward Pol's right wrist and plucked at the sleeve.

"Bare your forearm, if you please."

Pol reached across and did so.

Two fingers extended, Ibal traced the dragonmark. Then he chuckled and raised his eyes, staring at Pol, past him.

"It is as you say," he remarked. "I did not know of you—

© JUDY KING RIENIETS 81

though I see now that you are troubled by more than one lingering thing from out of Rondoval's past."

"That may well be," said Pol. "But how can you tell?"

"They circle you like swarms of bright insects," Ibal said, still looking past him.

Pol consciously shifted into his second mode of seeing, and while there were many strands in the vicinity, he detected nothing which resembled a circling swarm of insects.

"I fail to observe the phenomenon myself . . ."

"Most certainly," the other replied, "for it has doubtless been constantly with you—and it would of course seem different to you than it does to me, anyway, if you could detect it at all. You know how sorcerers' perceptions vary, and their emphasis upon different things."

Pol frowned.

"Or do you?" Ibal asked.

When Pol did not reply, the old sorcerer continued to stare, narrowing his eyes to tight slits.

"Now I am not so certain," he said. "At first I thought that the disorganization of your lights was a very clever disguise, but now—"

"My lights?" Pol said.

"With whom did you serve your apprenticeship—and when did you undergo initiation?" the other demanded.

Pol smiled.

"I grew up far from here," he replied, "in a place where things are not done that way."

"Ah, you are a Madwand! Preserve us from Madwands! Still . . . You are not *totally* disorganized—and anyone with that mark—" He nodded again at Pol's right arm. "—must possess an instinct for the Art. Interesting . . . So why do you travel to Belken?"

"To learn . . . some things."

The old sorcerer chuckled.

"And I go for self-indulgence," he said. "Call me Ibal, and accompany me. It will be good to have someone strange to talk with. —Your man is not a brother of the Art?"

"No, and Mouseglove is not really my man—he is my companion."

"Mouseglove, did you say? I seem to have heard that name before. Something to do with jewels, perhaps?"

"I am not a jeweler," Mouseglove replied hastily.

"No matter. Tomorrow I will tell you some things that may be of interest to you, Detson. But it is still over half a league to the place where I intend to camp. Let us move on. Upward! Forward!"

The servants raised the litter and moved ahead with it. Pol and Mouseglove took up positions behind it and followed.

That night they camped amid the ruins of what might once have been a small amphitheatre. Pol lay troubled for a long while, in fear of the dreams that might come to him. He still had not spoken of these, for in daytime the things of sleep seemed far away. But when the stillness descended and the fire dwindled the deeper places of shadow seemed filled with faces, as if some ghostly audience capable of seeing beyond the cowl of sleep had come together here to watch his journey into the place of baleful lights and screaming winds and cruelty. He shuddered and listened for a long time, his eyes darting. He knew of no magic to affect the content of his dreams. And he wondered again as to their significance, partly with the mind of one whose culture would have seen them in psychopathological terms, partly with the freshly tuned awareness that in this place another explanation could as readily apply. Then his thoughts began to drift, back to the encounter with the sorcerer who had tried to kill him at Rondoval. The dreams had begun almost immediately after that, and he wondered whether there could be a connection. Had the other laid a spell upon him before he had died, to trouble his sleep thereafter? His mind moved away, lulled by the steady creaking of insects in the distant wood. He wondered what Mark would have done. Looked for some drug to block it all out, perhaps. His mind drifted again . . .

The movement. Now a familiar thing. The fear was gone. There was only anticipation within the rapid and disjointed series of images by which he moved. There was the Gate, and . . .

It stopped. Everything stopped. He was frozen before the image of the partly opened Gate. It was fading, insubstantial, going away, and there was a hand upon his shoulder. He wanted to cry out, but only for a moment.

"It's all right now," came a whisper, and the hand left him.

Pol tried to turn his head, to sit up. He found that he could not stir. A large man, his face more than half-hidden in the shadow of his cowl, was rising from a kneeling position beside him, passing through his field of vision. Pol thought that he glimpsed part of a pale moustache and—impossibly—a shining, capped tooth.

"Then why can't I move?" he whispered through clenched teeth.

"It was far easier for me to lay a general spell upon this entire camp than to be selective about it. Then I needed but arouse you and leave the others unconscious. The paralysis is, unfortunately, a part of it."

Pol suspected that this was a lie but saw no way to test it.

"I saw that your sleep was troubled. I decided to grant you some relief."

"How can you see that a man's sleep is troubled?"

"I am something of a specialist in that matter which confronts you."

"That being . . . ?"

"Did your dream not involve a large door?"

Pol was silent for a moment. Then, "Yes," he said. "It did. How could you know this unless you induced it yourself?"

"I did not cause your dream. I did not even come here for purposes of releasing you from it."

"What, then?"

"You journey to Belken."

"You seem to know everything . . ."

"Do not be impertinent. As our interests may be conjoined, I am trying to help you. I understand more than you do about some of the forces which are influencing you. You make a serious mistake, wandering about the world announcing yourself at this point in your career. Now, I have just taken great pains to remove the memory of your name and origin from the minds of Ibal and everyone in his party. In the morning, he will only recall you as a Madwand traveling to Belken. Even your appearance will be a confusion to him. If he should ask your name again, have another one ready, and use it in Belken, also. Rondoval still has its enemies."

"I gathered something of this with the attempt on my life."

"When was this? Where?"

"A little over a week ago. Back home."

"I was not aware of this. Then it has begun. You should be safe for a time, if you remain incognito. I am going to rinse your hair with a chemical I have here, to conceal that white streak. It is too distinctive. And then we must hide your dragonmark."

"How?"

"A relatively simple matter. How do you see manifestations of the Powers when you are working a spell?"

Pol felt moisture upon his scalp.

"Usually as colored strands—threads, strings, cords."

"Interesting. Very well, then. You can imagine me as wrapping your forearm with flesh-colored strands—so closely as to entirely mask the mark. It will in no way interfere with your workings. When you wish to uncover it you need but go through an unwrapping ritual."

Pol felt his arm taken, raised.

"Who are you?" he asked. "How do you know all these things?"

"I am the sorcerer who should never have been, and mine is a peculiar link with your House."

"We are related?"

"No. Not even friends."

"Then why are you helping me?"

"I feel that your continued existence may serve me. There. Your arm is nicely disguised."

"If you really wish to protect me from something, you might do well to tell me somewhat about it."

"I do not deem that the most fitting course of action. First, nothing may happen to you, in which case I would have exposed you to information I'd rather not. Second, ignorance on your part may actually benefit me."

"Mister, someone's already gotten my number. I don't like the notion of being suddenly engaged in another sorcerous duel."

"Oh, they're all right if you win. That was the nature of the assassination attempt?"

"Yes."

"Well, you're still intact."

"Just barely."

"Good enough, my boy. Keeps you alert. Now, perhaps we'd best coarsen your features a bit and lighten your eyes a trifle. Shall we have a wart beside your nose? No? An interesting scar on your cheek then? Yes, that should do it . . ."

"And you won't give me your name?"

"It would mean nothing to you, but your knowledge of it might trouble me later."

Pol willed the dragonmark to life, hoping his disguised arm would mask this from the other's second sight. The man voiced no reaction as the throbbing began. Pol sent the force up and down

his right arm, freeing it from the paralysis. Then his neck. He had
to be able to turn his head a bit . . . Best to leave the rest as it
was for the moment. Catalepsy, he knew, is hard to fake.

The hands continued to move over his face. The other's face
remained out of his field of vision. Pol summoned a tough, gray
strand and felt its ghostly presence across his fingertips.

"Now they'll all think you've been to Heidelberg . . ."

"What," Pol asked him, "did you say?"

"An obscure reference," the other offered quickly. "A really
good sorcerer has knowledge of places beyond this place, you
know—"

Pol let the energy pulse through him, breaking the paralysis entirely. He rolled onto his side and directed a flash movement of
the gray strand. It snaked upward and snared the man's wrists. As
he tightened it, he began to rise.

"Now I will ask my questions again," Pol stated.

"Fool of a Madwand!" said the other.

The strand writhed in Pol's hand and a feeling like an electrical
shock traveled up his arm. He could not release the thing and the
dragonmark felt as if it were on fire. He opened his mouth to
scream, but nothing came out.

"You are very lucky," was the last thing he heard the man say
before the storm reached his brain and he fell.

Dawn had just bruised the eastern heaven when he opened his
eyes. It was the voices of Ibal's servants which had awakened him,
as they moved about packing their gear, making ready to decamp.
Pol raised his hands to his temples, trying to recall how much he
had drunk . . .

"Who are you? Where's Pol?"

He turned his head, saw Mouseglove standing arms akimbo,
staring at him.

"Is there a scar on my cheek?" he asked, raising his fingertips
to search it.

"Yes."

"Listen to my voice. Don't you recognize it? Is the streak in my
hair gone, too?"

"Oh . . . I see. Yes, it is. Why a disguise at this point?"

Pol got up and began gathering his things.

"I'll tell you about it while we're walking along."

He searched the ground for signs of his visitor, but it was a
rocky place and there were none. As they followed Ibal's servitors

back toward the trail, Mouseglove paused and pointed into a clump of withered shrubbery.

"What do you make of that?" he asked.

Three mummified rabbits hung among the tangle of branches. Shaking his head, Pol walked on.

III.

It was more than a little traumatic at the beginning: the sights and sounds—all of the new things we encountered beyond Rondoval. I hovered close to Pol for the first several days, drifting along, sensing everything within range, familiarizing myself with the laws governing new groups of phenomena. Travel, I discovered, *is* broadening, for I found myself spreading over a larger area as time went on. My little joke. I realized that my expansion was at least partly attributable to the increased number of things whose essences I absorbed as we traveled along—plants as well as animals, though the latter were more to my liking—and partly in accord with Boyle's and Charles' laws, which I'd picked out of Pol's mind one evening when he returned in memory to his university days. I cannot, in all honesty, consider myself a gas. Though I am anchored to the physical plane, I am not entirely manifested here and can withdraw partly with ease, entirely with more difficulty. I confine myself to a given area and move about by means of my will. I am not certain how that works either. I was aware, however, that my total volume was increasing and that my ability to do physical things was improving—like the rabbits. I had decided to look upon the entire journey as an educational experience. Any new thing that I learned might ultimately have some bearing upon my quest for identity and purpose.

And I was learning new things, some of them most peculiar. For instance, when that cloaked and muffled man entered the compound, I had felt a rippling as of a gentle breeze, only it was not physical; I had heard something like a low note and seen a mass of swimming colors. Then everyone, including the camp watchman, was asleep. There followed more movements and colors and sounds. Having recently learned the meaning of "subjective", I can safely say that that is what they were, rather than tangible. Then I observed with interest as he altered the sleepers' memories concerning Pol, realizing from the sensations I had experienced and from my memory of those back at Rondoval during

Pol's duel with the sorcerer in brown that I was extremely sensitive to magical emanations. I felt as if I could easily have altered these workings. I saw no reason to do so, however, so I merely observed. From my small knowledge of such affairs, it seemed that this one had an unusual style in the way he shifted forces among the planes. Yes. Sudden memories of a violent occasion reinforced this impression. He was peculiar, but I could see how he did everything that he did.

Then he stood beside Pol for a long while and I could not tell what he was about. He was employing some power different from that which he had used minutes before, and I did not understand it. Something within me jerked spasmodically when he reached out and laid a hand upon Pol's shoulder. Why, I did not know, but I moved nearer. I witnessed the entire conversation and the transformation of Pol's appearance. When the man covered the dragon-mark I found myself wanting to cry out, "No!" But, of course, I had no voice. It irritated me considerably to see it done, though I knew that it remained intact beneath the spell—and I was aware that Pol could undo the spell whenever he chose. What this reaction told me about myself, I could not say.

But then, when Pol rose and there was a brief and rapid exchange of forces between the men, I rushed to settle upon Pol and permeate his form, inspecting it for damage. I could discover nothing which seemed permanently debilitating to his kind, and since they generally render themselves unconscious during the night I made no effort to interfere with this state.

Withdrawing, I then set out to locate the other man. I was not certain why, nor what I would do should I succeed in finding him. But he had departed quickly and there was no trace of him about, so the questions remained academic.

That was when I came across the rabbits and terminated them, as well as the bush where they crouched. I felt immediately stronger. I puzzled over all my reactions and the more basic questions which lay behind them—wondering, too, whether I was really made for such a fruitless function as introspection.

No one in the company, Ibal included, seemed to take note of Pol's altered appearance. And none addressed him by name. It was as if each of them had forgotten it and was embarrassed to reveal the fact to the others. Eventually, those who spoke with him settled upon "Madwand" as a term of address, and Pol did not even get to use the other name he had ready. Conceding the possibility of its protective benefit, he was nevertheless irritated that his new identity had caused Ibal to forget whatever it was that he had intended telling him about Rondoval. Not knowing how strong the stranger's memory-clouding spell might be, he was loath to associate himself with Rondoval in his companions' minds by broaching the subject himself.

It was two nights later, as they sat to dinner, that Ibal raised a matter almost as interesting.

"So, Madwand, tell me of your plans," he said, spooning something soft and mushy between what remained of his teeth. "What do you propose doing at the fest?"

"Learning," Pol replied. "I would like to meet some fellow practitioners, and I would like to become more proficient in the Art."

Ibal chuckled moistly.

"Why don't you just come out and say that you're looking for a sponsor for initiation?" he asked.

"Would I be eligible?" Pol inquired.

"If a master would back you."

"What would the benefits be?"

Ibal shook his head.

"I find it hard to believe you are that naive. Where did you grow up?"

"In a place where the question never arose."

"I suppose I can believe that if I try, since you *are* a Madwand. All right. I occasionally find ignorance very refreshing. Proper experience of the rituals involved in initiation will result in an ordering of your lights. This will allow you to handle greater quantities of the energy that moves through all things. It will permit you to grow in power, a thing which might not happen otherwise."

"Will initiations actually be conducted at Belken this time, during the course of the gathering?"

"Yes. I plan on having Nupf initiated there—though Suhuy, I feel, is not ready."

He gestured toward the larger of his apprentices, the youth with dark eyes and pale hair. Suhuy frowned and looked away.

"Once an apprentice has been initiated he is on his own, so to speak?" Pol asked.

"Yes, though a man will occasionally remain with his master for a period of time afterwards to learn certain fine points of the Art which might have been neglected while he was studying the basics."

"Well, if I can't locate a sponsor I guess that I'll just have to muddle through life on my own."

"If you are aware of the dangers of initiation . . ."

"I'm not."

"Death and madness are the main ones. Every now and then they claim a few who were not quite ready."

"Could I get some coaching so as not to be unready?"

"That could be arranged."

"Then I'd be willing."

"In that case, I will sponsor you in return for future goodwill. It's always nice to have a few friends in the trade."

The dreams of the Gate and the peculiar land beyond them did not return that night, nor on any succeeding night until their arrival at the festival. The days passed uneventfully, routinely, as they hiked along, until only the fact of his changed appearance assured Pol that something unusual had actually occurred. The terrain had altered as they headed upward, though the ascent here was more gradual than the descent from the mountains about Rondoval. Belken itself was a great, black, fang-like peak, dotted with numerous depressions, bare of trees. The evening they first caught sight of it, it seemed outlined by a faint white light. Mouseglove drew Pol aside and they halted to regard it.

"Are you sure you know what you're getting into?" he asked him.

"Ibal has outlined the initiation procedures for me," Pol replied, "and he's given me an idea of what to expect at the various stations."

"That is not exactly what I had in mind," Mouseglove said.

"What, then?"

"A sorcerer tried to kill you back at Rondoval. Another came by, apparently to help you, last week. I get the impression that you are in the middle of something nasty and magical—and here you go, walking right into a den of magicians and about to attempt something dangerous without the normal preparations."

"On the other hand," Pol replied, "it is probably the best place for me to discover what is going on. And I'm sure I will find uses for any additional insight and strength the initiation provides."

"Do you really trust Ibal?"

Pol shrugged.

"It seems that I have to, up to a point."

"Unless you decide to quit the whole game right now."

"That would put me right back where I started. No thanks."

"It would give you time to think things over more, perhaps find a different line of investigation to follow."

"Yes," Pol answered, "I wish that I could. But time, I feel, is something I cannot afford to spend so freely."

Mouseglove sighed and turned away.

"That mountain looks sinister," he said.

"I have to agree with you."

The following morning, proceeding among the foothills, they reached the top of a low ridge and the group halted. Spread out before the eastern base of the mountain was something out of dreamland or fairy tale: a sparkling collection of creamy towers and golden spires amid buildings which looked as if they had been carved out of massive gemstones; there were bright arches over glistening roadways, columns of jet, rainbow-hung fountains . . .

"Gods!" Pol said. "I'd no idea it was anything like that!"

He heard Ibal chuckle.

"What's funny?" Pol asked.

"One is only young once. Let it be a surprise," the old sorcerer replied.

Puzzled, Pol continued on. As the day advanced, the dream-city lost some of its glamour. First went the sparkling and the rainbows; then the colors began to fade. A haziness came over the buildings, and within it a uniform grayness settled upon the entire prospect. The structures seemed to diminish in size, and some of the spires and higher columns vanished altogether. Glassy walls grew opaque and took on motion, a gentle, flapping movement. Then the fountains and the archways were gone. It was as if he now looked upon the place through a dimming and distorting glass.

When they sat to lunch, Pol addressed Ibal:

"All right, I'm surprised and I'm several hours older now. What's become of the city?"

Ibal nearly choked on his mush.

"No, no," he finally said. "Wait until dinnertime. Watch the show."

And so he did. As the sun moved westward and the shadow of the peak fell over the hazy outlines of the structures at its base, the flapping movement ceased and the walls began to acquire something of their former sheen. Pol and Mouseglove continued to stare as they approached. As the shadows lengthened, the place seemed to grow, slowly at first, more rapidly as the afternoon faded toward evening. The haze itself seemed to be dimming and the outline of higher structures again became visible within it. Drawing nearer to it, they became aware of the spurting of fountains. The colors gradually reappeared within the still-firming outlines of the buildings. The towers, columns and arches took on a greater solidity.

By dinnertime they were very near, and the city was much closer to its early morning appearance. The haze continued to dissipate as they sat watching it, taking their meal.

"Well, have you guessed?" Ibal asked, spooning in a dark broth.

"It appears to be different things at different times," Pol said. "So obviously it is not what it seems and must represent some sort of enchantment. I've no idea what's really there, or why it changes."

"What is really there is a group of caves, shacks and tents," Ibal explained. "Each time, by lot, various practitioners acquire the responsibility for putting the place into order for the gathering. What they normally do is send their apprentices and some servants on ahead. These clean and repair the structures, raise the tents and set up the various facilities. Then the apprentices usually vie in working out spells to give it a pleasing appearance. However, apprentices vary in ability, and since the thing is only to be temporary first class spells are seldom employed. Consequently, it is beautiful from evening through dawn. As the day progresses, however, it begins to waver. Things are weakest at noon, and then you catch glimpses of what is really behind it all."

"Do the spells hold on the inside as well as the outside?"

"Indeed, Madwand, they do. You shall see for yourself soon."

As they watched, the sparkling began again, faint at first, growing.

They reached the foot of Belken by evening and entered the bright city which had grown up there. The first archway through which they passed might have been made of branches strapped together, but it gave every appearance of gold-veined marble possessed of intricate carvings. Countless lights drifted through the air at several times the height of a man. Pol kept turning his head, assessing the wonders. Unlike any city with which he was familiar, this one seemed clean. The way beneath their feet was unnaturally bright. The buildings appeared almost fragile, with an eggshell translucence to them. Filigreed screens covered fancifully shaped

windows in walls sporting designs of glowing gemstones. There
were balconies and overhead walkways, arcades through which
richly garbed men and women passed. Open-fronted shops displayed magical paraphernalia and exotic beasts were penned and
tethered throughout the city—though a few wandered harmlessly,
as if taking in the sights themselves. Thick clouds of red smoke
rose from a brazier on a corner where a turbanned mage chanted,
a demonic face and form taking shape within it high above the
street. The sounds of flutes, stringed instruments and drums came
from several directions. On an impulse, Pol jerked his guitar into
existence, tuned it, slung it and began playing as they walked
along. He felt his dragonmark throbbing invisibly, as if in response to the magical ambiance they were entering. Bright birds in
cages of silver and gold trilled responses to his song. A few of the
passing faces turned his way. High above, the face of the mountain
was glowing softly, as if traversed by swarms of fireflies. And even
higher, the stars had appeared in a clear sky. Cool breezes moved
about him, bringing the odors of exotic incenses, perfumes, of
sweet logs burning.

Mouseglove sniffed and listened, fingers twitching, eyes darting.

"It would be difficult to know what to steal, in a place where
nothing is what it seems," he remarked.

"Then you might look upon it as a vacation."

"Hardly," Mouseglove replied, eyeing a demon-face which
seemed to regard him from behind a grating high in the wall to his
left. "Perhaps as an experience in compulsory education . . ."

Ibal, croaking orders to his servants at every turn, seemed to
know the way to his quarters. They were, Pol later learned, the
same apartments he had always occupied. Their appearance would
be radically altered upon each occasion, one of the older servants
informed him. Orientation here was a matter of familiarity with
position rather than appearance.

The apartments to which they were conducted as Ibal's guests
seemed extensive and elegant, though the eye-swindling shimmer
of glamourie lay upon everything and Pol noted that solid-appear-
ing walls seemed to yield somewhat if he leaned upon them,
smooth floors were sometimes uneven to the feet and chairs were
never as comfortable as they looked.

Ibal had dismissed them, saying that he intended to rest and
that he would introduce them to the initiation officials on the morrow. So, after bathing and changing their garments, Pol and
Mouseglove went out to see more of the town.

The balls of white light illuminated the major thoroughfares. Globes of various colors drifted above the lesser ways. They passed knots of youths whose overheard conversations were like the ruminations of philosophers and groups of old men who called upon their powers to engage in practical jokes—such as the tiny cloud hovering just beneath an archway which suddenly rattled and drenched anyone who passed below it, to the accompaniment of uproarious laughter from the gnome-like masters lurking in the shadows.

Brushing away the moisture, Pol and Mouseglove continued on to a narrow stair leading down to a winding street less well illuminated than those above—blue and red lights, smaller and dimmer than the others, moving slowly above it.

"That looks to be a possibly interesting way," Mouseglove indicated, leaning on a railing above it.

"Let's go down and have a look."

It seemed a place of refreshment. Establishments serving food and beverage, both indoors and out, lined the way. They strolled slowly by all of them, then turned and started back again.

"I like the looks of that one," said Mouseglove, gesturing to the right. "One of the empty tables under the canopy, perhaps, where we can watch the people pass."

"Good idea," said Pol, and they made their way over and sat down.

A small, dark, smiling man wearing a green Kaftan emerged from the establishment's doorway almost immediately.

"And what will the gentlemen have?" he inquired.

"I'd like a glass of red wine," said Pol.

"Make mine white and almost sour," said Mouseglove.

The man turned away and immediately turned back. He held a tray bearing two glasses of wine, one light, one dark.

"Useful trick, that," Mouseglove observed.

"Private spell," the other replied.

The man grew almost apologetic then as he asked them to drop their payment through a small hoop into a basket.

"All the others are starting it, too," he said. "Too many enchanted pebbles going around. You might even have some without knowing it."

But their coins remained coins as they passed through the charmed circle.

"We just arrived," Pol told him.

"Well, keep an eye out for stones."

He moved off to take another order.

The wine was extremely good, though Pol suspected that a part of its taste was enchantment. Still, he reflected after a time, what difference should it make? Like the entire place about them—if it serves its purpose, appearance can be far more important than content.

"Hardly an original observation," Mouseglove replied when he voiced it. "And it meant a lot to me every time I lifted a bogus jewel I thought was real."

Pol chuckled.

"Then it served its purpose."

Mouseglove laughed.

"All right. All right. But when death gets involved it is better to know which is the real dagger and which the real hand. After what happened that last night in your library, I would be very careful in a place like this."

"By what means that I am not already employing?"

"Well, that magical shower we passed through earlier," Mouse-glove began. "I just noticed—"

He was interrupted by the approach of a blond, well-built young man with finely chiseled features and a flashing smile. He was extravagantly dressed and he moved with an extraordinary grace and poise.

"Madwand! And Mouseglove! Strange meeting you here! Waiter! Another of whatever they're having for my friends! And a glass of your best for me!"

He drew up a chair and seated himself at their table.

"It looks as if they did a better than usual job this year," he said, gesturing. "How do you like your accommodations?"

"Uh—fine," Pol replied as the waiter arrived and produced their drinks.

The youth gestured and his hand was suddenly filled with coins. They leapt upward from it, arched through the hoop and into the basket with a small pyrotechnic display.

"Colorful," Pol said. "Listen, I hate to seem rude since you're buying, but I can't seem to recall . . ."

The youth laughed, his handsome features creasing with merriment.

"Of course not, of course not," he said. "I am Ibal, and you are looking at the finest rejuvenation spell ever wrought." He brushed a speck of dust from his bright sleeve. "Not to mention a few cosmetic workings," he added softly.

"Really!"

"Amazing!"

"Yes. I am ready to meet once again with my beloved Vonnie, for two weeks of lovemaking, revelry, good food and drink. It is the only reason I still come to these things."

"How—interesting."

"Yes. We first met here nearly three hundred years ago, and our feelings have remained undiminished across the centuries."

"Impressive," Pol said. "But do you not see one another in between times?"

"Gods, no! If we had to live together on a day-to-day basis one of us would doubtless kill the other. Two weeks every four years is just right." He stared into his drink a moment before raising it to his lips. "Besides," he added, "we spend a lot of the intervening time recovering."

He looked up again.

"Madwand, what have you done to yourself?"

"What do you mean?" Pol asked.

"That white streak in your hair. Why is it there?"

Pol ran a hand through his still-moist thatch.

"Little joke," he said.

"Not in the best of taste," said Ibal, shaking his head. "You'll have people associating you with Det's Disaster. Ahh!"

They followed a sudden movement of his gaze out along the street, past a halted fat man and a pair of strollers, to where a woman approached under a swaying blue light. She was of medium height, her hair long and dark and glossy, her form superbly molded beneath a light, clinging costume, her features delicate, lovely, smiling.

Following his sharp intake of breath, Ibal rose to his feet. Pol and Mouseglove did the same.

"Gentlemen, this is Vonnie," he announced as she came up to the table. He embraced her, kept his arm about her. "My dear, you are lovelier than ever. These are my friends, Madwand and Mouseglove. Let us have a drink with them before we go our way."

She nodded to them as he brought her a chair.

"It is good to meet you," she said. "Have you come very far?" and Pol, captivated by the charm of her voice as well as the freshness of her person, felt a sudden and acute loneliness.

He forgot his reply as soon as he uttered it, and he spent the next several minutes admiring her.

As they rose to leave, Ibal leaned forward and whispered, "The hair—I'm serious. You'd best correct it soon, or the initiation officials may think you flippant. At any other time, of course, it would not matter. But in one seeking initiation—well, it is not a time for joking, if you catch my meaning."

Pol nodded, wondering at the simplest way to deal with it.

"I'll take care of it this evening."

"Very good. I will see you some time tomorrow—not too early."

"Enjoy yourselves."

Ibal smiled.

"I'm sure."

Pol watched them go, then returned his attention to his drink.

"Don't look suddenly," Mouseglove whispered through unmoving lips, "but there is a fat man who has been loitering across the way for some time now."

"I'd sort of noticed," Pol replied, sweeping his gaze over the bulky man's person as he raised his glass. "What about him?"

"I know him," Mouseglove said, "or knew him—professionally. His name is Ryle Merson."

Pol shook his head.

"The name means nothing to me."

"He is the sorcerer I once mentioned. It was over twenty years ago that he hired me to steal those seven statuettes from your father."

Pol felt a strong urge to turn and stare at the large man in gold and gray. He restrained himself.

". . . And there was no hint from him as to what he wanted them for?" he asked.

"No."

"I feel they're very safe—in with my guitar," Pol said.

When he did look again, Ryle Merson was talking with a tall man who wore a long-sleeved black tunic, red trousers and high black boots, a red bandana about his head. The man had his back to them, but a little later he turned and his eyes met Pol's in passing, before the two of them moved on slowly up the street.

"What about that one?"

Mouseglove shook his head.

"For a moment I thought there was something familiar about him, but no—I don't know his name and I can't say where I might have seen him before, if indeed I did."

"Is this a coincidence, I wonder?"

"Ryle is a sorcerer, and this is a sorcerers' convention."

"Why do you think he chose to stand there for so long?"

"It could be that he was simply waiting for his friend," Mouseglove said, "though I found myself wondering whether he had recognized me."

"It's been a long time," Pol said.

"Yes."

"He could simply have come over and spoken with you if he wanted to be certain who you were."

"True."

Mouseglove raised his drink.

"Let's finish up and get out of here," he said.

"Okay."

Later, the edge gone from the evening, they returned to their apartments. Not entirely because Mouseglove had suggested it, Pol wove an elaborate series of warning spells about the place and slept with a blade beside the bed.

IV.

Enough of philosophical rumination! I decided. It is all fruitless, for I am still uncertain as to everything concerning my existence. A philosopher is a dead poet and a dying theologian—I got that from Pol's mind one night. I am not certain where Pol got it, but it bore the proper cast of contempt to match my feelings. I had grown tired of thinking about my situation. It was time that I did something.

I found the city at Belken's foot to be unnerving, but stimulating as well. Rondoval was not without its share of magic—from utilitarian workings and misunderstood enchantments to forgotten spells waiting to go off and a lot of new stuff Pol had left lying about. But this place was a veritable warehouse of magic—spell overlying spell, many of them linked, a few in conflict, new ones being laid at every moment and old ones dismantled. The spells at Rondoval were old, familiar things which I knew well how to humor. Here the power hummed or shone all about me constantly —some of it most strange, some even threatening—and I never knew but that I might be about to collide with a deadly, unsuspected force. This served to heighten my alertness if not my awareness. Then, too, I seemed to draw more power into myself just by virtue of moving amid such large concentrations of it.

The first indication that I might be able to question someone concerning my own status came when we entered the city and I beheld the being in the tower of red fumes. I watched it until the manifestation dissipated, and then was pleased to note that the creature assumed a form similar to my own. I approached the receding thing immediately and directed an inquiry toward it.

"What are you?" I asked.

"An errand boy," it replied. "I was stupid enough to let someone find out my name."

"I do not understand."

"I'm a demon just like you. Only I'm doing time. Go ahead and mock me. But maybe someday you'll get yours."

"I really do not understand."

"I haven't the time to explain. I have to fetch enough ice from the mountaintop to fill all the chests in the food lockers. My accursèd master has one of the concessions here."

"I'll help you," I said, "if you'll show me what to do—and if you will answer my questions as we work."

"Come on, then. To the peak."

I followed.

As we passed through the middle reaches of the air, I inquired, "I'm a demon, too, you say?"

"I guess so. I can't think of too many other things that give the same impression."

"Name one, if you can."

"Well, an elemental—but they're too stupid to ask questions the way you do. You've got to be a demon."

We got to the top where I learned how to manage the ice. It proved to be a simple variation on the termination/absorption techniques I employed on living creatures.

As we swirled back down toward the lockers—as two great spinning towers of glittering crystals—I asked, "Where do we come from? My memory doesn't go back all that far."

"We are assembled out of the universal energy flux in a variety of fashions. One of the commonest ways is for a powerful sorcerous agency to call one of us into being to perform some specific task—tailor-making us, so to speak. In the process we are named, and customarily we are released once the job is finished. Only, if some lesser or lazier mage—such as my accursèd master—later learns your name he might bind you to his service and your freedom ends again. That is why you will find quite a few of us doing jobs for which we are not ideally suited. There just aren't that many top-notch sorcerers around—and some of them even grow lazy, or are often in a hurry. Ah, if only my accursèd master could be induced to make but the smallest mistake in one of his charging rituals!"

"What would happen then?"

"Why, I'd be freed in that moment to tear the son of a bitch apart and take off on my own, hoping that he had left no magical document mentioning my name nor passed it along to some snot-nosed apprentice. To be safe, you should always destroy your accursèd former master's quarters to take care of any such paperwork—burning is usually best—and then go after any apprentices who might be in the vicinity."

"I'll remember that," I said, as we reformed our burdens into large chunks in the lockers and headed back for more.

"But you've never had this problem? Not even once?"

"No. Not at all."

"Unusual. Perhaps you had your origin in some massive natural disaster. That sometimes happens."

"I don't remember anything like that. I do seem to recall a lot of fighting, but that is hardly the same thing."

"Hm. Lots of blood?"

"I suppose so. Will that do it?"

"I don't think so, not just by itself. But it could help if something else had started the process."

"I think there was a bad storm, also."

"Storms can help, too. But even so, that's not enough."

"Well, what should I do?"

"Do? Be thankful that no one knows your name."

"*I* don't even know my name—that is, if I have one at all."

We reached the peak, acquired another load, began the return trip.

"You must have a name. Everything does. One of the old ones told me that."

"Old ones?"

"You really are naive, aren't you? The old ones are the ancient demons from the days that men have forgotten, ages ago. Fortunately for them, their names have also been forgotten, so that they dwell largely untroubled by sorcerers, in distant grottoes, upon far peaks, in the hearts of volcanoes, in places at the ocean's bottom. To hear them tell it, no accurséd master could oppress you like the accurséd masters of long ago. It is difficult to know whether there really is any difference, since I know of none so unfortunate as to have served under both ancient and modern accurséd masters. The old ones are wise, though, just from having been around for so long. One of them might be able to help you."

"You actually know some of them?"

"Oh yes! During one of my intervals of freedom I dwelled among them far below, in the Grottoes of the Growling Earth, where the hot magma surges and steams—a most wondrous and happy place! Would that I were there now!"

"Why don't you return?"

"Nothing would please me more. But I am bound not to wander too far by my accurséd master's accurséd spell, and he is not in the habit of granting vacations."

"How unfortunate."

"Indeed."

We entered the lockers again and finished filling the ice chests. "Now, thanks to you, I am finished ahead of schedule," the demon said, "and my accurséd master will not summon me to another accurséd task until he realizes that this one is finished. Therefore, I have a few minutes of freedom. If you would like, we will return to the heights where we can see for a great distance and I will attempt to give you directions for reaching the Grottoes of the Growling Earth—though their entrance lies on another continent."

"Show me the way," I said, and he soared upward.

I followed.

The instructions were complicated, but I set out immediately to follow them. I fled far to the northwest until I came to a great water heaving regularly toward the stars it imaged. There, unaccountably, I slowed. I knew that I had to cross it as the next stage of my journey, but I was drained of all will to begin. I drifted northward along the coastline, puzzled. What was it that was holding me back?

Finally, I sought full control of my nebulous person. I attempted to consider the situation in a totally rational manner. I saw no reason for hesitation. I ignored the strange lethargy which had taken hold of me. Forcing myself forward, I passed over a narrow, pebbly strand of beach and on out above the splashing swells.

I felt my new resolve waver almost immediately, yet I struggled to continue, to break through whatever odd barrier it was that had been raised against me.

It was then that I heard the voice, mixed in with the booming of the surf.

"Bell, or," it said. "Bell, or . . ."

And I listened and grew afraid.

"Bell, or," it repeated, "bell, or, bell, or, bell, or," over and over again.

I realized that some part of me had immediately understood something of what lay behind those utterances. And I knew they meant that I was defeated in my quest.

I summoned my last bit of will to oppose the force which held me, for here at last was something I might query.

"Why?" I hurled at the waves and the sky. "Why? What is it that you want of me?"

There was a moment of silence, and then the voice returned: "Bell, or, bell, or . . ."

I felt defeat wash through me, a dark, cold thing like the waters below, as I saw that those strange words were to be my only answer.

Turning, I rushed back to the shore then fled southward, knowing I would have to look elsewhere for my answers. The words faded gradually within my being. My thoughts became focussed upon Pol Detson.

Once I reached glowing Belken and the magic-infested city at its foot, I proceeded unerringly to the building and the room where Pol lay sleeping. How I achieved this with no real effort, I could not say, unless some bond had grown between us as a result of our association.

As I inspected the defenses he had reared, I heard him moan softly. I entered his sleeping mind and saw that he had passed beyond a door in his dreams into a place which both delighted and repelled him. I had never intervened in his affairs before, but I recalled that he had seemed to be relieved when awakened by the nameless sorcerer that last time he had dreamed such a dream. So I caused him to awaken.

He lay there for a long while, troubled, then drifted into a more peaceful slumber. I departed then to seek my demon acquaintance and see whether there was anything else I might learn.

I drifted over to the accursèd master's quarters, but my friend was neither there nor in the vicinity. Then, faintly, I detected the glittering trail such as had occurred behind us during the ice-hauling expeditions. I hurried to follow, as it had faded further even as I had considered it.

I sped along the skiey trail as rapidly as I could conduct myself. The distance proved to be great, but a slight brightening of the way indicated that I was gaining.

Many leagues farther to the south and the west, the trail arced downward toward a riverside town. It ended at a house which was vibrating and from which a series of crashing noises could be heard. I passed into the place and noted that blood was smeared everywhere—the walls, the floors, even the ceiling. My friend had hold of a male human whose limbs were broken and whose brains had been dashed out against the fireplace.

"Greetings! You're back so soon! Was there some problem with my directions?"

"No, but some force I do not understand prevented me from departing this continent."

"Strange."

The human flew across the room to crash against the far wall.

"Do you know what I think it is?"

"No. What?" I said.

"I believe you are under a spell that you do not even know about—bound in a particular way to some very special duty."

"I have no idea what it could be."

"Give me a hand with the entrails, will you? They should be strung about."

"Sure."

"Well, I think that you ought to find out what the thing is and discharge it. Maybe the accursed master who laid it on you is dead now or demented. In either case, you're very lucky. Once you've done whatever there is to be done, you'll be free."

"How do I find out what it is?"

"I guess that I am going to have to instruct you further in these matters. Since I am prepared to count you as a friend, I am going to tell you something in strictest confidence—my name. It is Galleran."

"That's a nice name," I said.

"It is more than just a word. It summarizes me when it is fully understood."

We finished the stringing and Galleran dismembered the body, passing me a leg and an arm.

"Do something artistic with these."

I hung one over a rafter and placed the other in a large kettle.

"Because I know my name I know all that there is to know about me," Galleran said. "You will, too, as you begin to understand it. Now, what you must do is discover your own name. When you learn that, it will also bring you knowledge of the task with which you have been charged."

"Really?"

"Certainly. It must follow."

Galleran placed the head upon the mantelpiece.

"How am I to find it out?" I asked.

"You must search your earliest memories—many times, perhaps. It is there, somewhere. When you find it you will know it. When you know it, you will know yourself. Then you can act."

"I will—try," I said.

Galleran proceeded to strew embers from the fireplace about the room.

"Help me to fan these to flame now, will you? It is always best to leave the place burning after your work is done."

"Surely."

As we strove to set the room to fire, I asked, "Why is it that your accursèd master wanted this man destroyed?"

"One of them owed the other money, I believe, and did not wish to pay it. I forget which."

"Oh."

We waited about until we saw that we had a good blaze going. Then we rose into the night with the smoke and headed back toward Belken.

"Thank you for all that you have taught me this day," I said as we parted later, "Galleran."

"I am glad to be of help. I must admit that you have roused my curiosity—mightily. Let me know when you have learned your story, will you?"

"Yes," I said. "I will do that."

Galleran returned to the accursèd master's quarters to report the completion of the assigned task. I rose into the air, heading toward a place high upon the western face of Belken. Earlier, on our ice-gathering expedition, I had noticed an opening there heading into the heart of the mountain, strange lights and vibrations all about it. I had grown very curious as to where it led and was determined to explore there. One never knows where one's name might lie.

V.

. . . Pol drifted again through the great Gate and into the land beyond. Moving more rapidly than in the past, he viewed another hunt, transformation and pursuit with growing amusement. On the second capture, however, the victim was cannibalized and another had to be sought. Pol experienced a psychic tugging which drew him away from the scene and on out across the wasteland. For what seemed to be days he traveled, in a dim, indeterminate form, over the unchanging deadlands, coming at last to a worn but high range of black mountains which extended from horizon to horizon. Three times he assailed its heights and three times he fell back; on the fourth occasion, the dry, howling winds forced him toward a gap through which he fled. He emerged on the other side above a terraced city which covered this entire face of the range. This slope, however, continued to a far lower level than that on the opposite side, dropping at last to the shore of an ancient, waveless, tideless sea and continuing on below its surface. Circling, he saw the outlines of buildings beneath the waters and the dark, moving forms of the beings who dwelled there. Through the always-evening haze, he saw the creatures of the upper terraces, gray, long-limbed, ogre-like, slightly smaller versions of the things he had seen in the wastes. Human-appearing beings also were there, moving freely among them.

He descended very slowly, coming to rest atop a high spire, where he perched and regarded the figures below. A great number of these congregated quickly at the base of the structure. After a time, they built a fire, brought forth a number of bound people, dismembered them and burned them. The smoke rose up, he breathed it, and it was pleasing to him.

Finally, he spread his wings and spiralled downward to where they waited upon the lowest terrace. They made obeisance to him and played him music upon instruments which wailed, thrummed and rattled. He strutted among them, occasionally choosing one to rend with his great beak and talons. Whenever he did this, the others watched with awe and obvious pleasure. Later, one who wore a brass collar studded with pale, smouldering stones approached, holding a three-pronged iron staff surmounted by a sooty white flame.

He followed the light and the one who bore it into the shadowy interior of one of the buildings—a lopsided metal structure of tilted floors and slanted walls. It was windowless and damp; it smelled of stale perfumes. Deep within the place, cold and still upon a high marble slab, lay the woman, candles burning at her head and her feet, her only garments garland and girdle of red flower petals already touched with brown. Her hair was a soft yellow verging upon white. Her lips, nipples and nails were painted blue. He uttered a soft trilling note and mounted the stair, the slab and the woman. Raking her once with claw and slashing her twice with his beak, he began to sing. He enfolded her then with his wings and began a slow movement. The one who bore the iron staff struck it in slow, regular rhythm upon the cold stone floor, its flame making dancing shadows upon the weeping walls.

After a long while, the woman opened her pale eyes, but they did not focus and she did not move until many minutes had passed. Then she began to smile.

When the three of them came forth, others had assembled and more were rising from the depths and moving downward from the higher levels. The thrumming, wailing, dry rattling of the music had grown to massive proportions, and a steady clicking sound which came from the chests of the assembled creatures themselves rose in counterpoint to it. Then began a slow procession, led by the light-bearer, which moved over many levels of the world-circling, sea-dipped city. They stayed in red chambers during their journey, and the sea changed color six times as they moved both above and beneath it. Massive russet worms swam to accompany their passage—eyeless, humming, streaked and rotating—and space was folded, that prospects came and went with great rapidity. The notes of a mighty gong preceded them and signed their departures.

The sky grew even darker on the day of his daughter's birth. Nascae tossed, moaned and cried out, afterwards lying as still and cold as she had that day upon her slab. The mountains shouted thunder and a red rain fell, flowing like waterfalls of blood down the terraces to the sea. The child was named Nyalith, to the sounds of tabor and bone flute. When she spread her wings and soared above the world there was a sound like thunder, and horns

of yellow light preceded her. She would rule them for ten thousand years.

He flew to the highest peak of the black range and turned himself to stone, there to await Talkne, Serpent of the Still Waters, who would come to contest the land of Qod with him. The people made pilgrimages to that place, and Nyalith offered sacrifices at his feet. Prodromolu, Father of the Age, Opener of the Way, they called him in tireless chant, bathing him in honey and spices, wine and blood.

He felt his spirit rise, singing, to flash beyond the mountains. Then the deadlands twisted and churned beneath him. He dropped through a fading night toward brightness.

Pol awoke with a feeling of well-being. He opened his eyes and regarded the window through which the morning light leaked. He drew a deep breath and flexed his muscles. A cup of steaming coffee would be delightful, he decided, knowing full well that such was not attainable upon this world. Not yet, anyway. It was on his list of things to look into when he had the chance. Now . . .

At that instant, his dream returned to him, and he saw it to be the source of his pleasure. With it came remembrance of other dreams of a similar nature, dreams—he realized now—which had come to him every night since the nameless sorcerer had visited him on the trail and changed his appearance. But these, unlike the others, were uniformly pleasant despite a certain grotesqueness.

He rose, to visit the latrine, to wash, to dress, to rinse the streak in his hair with a jar of liquid he had purchased from an apothecary on the way home the previous evening. While he was about these things, he heard Mouseglove stirring. He dismantled the warning spells while he waited for the man to ready himself. Then the two of them stopped by Ibal's quarters but were told by a servant that the master could not be disturbed.

"Then let's take a walk and find some breakfast," Mouseglove suggested.

Pol nodded, and they made their way back to the small street with the cafes. The night's sparkle and sheen faded as they dined; and as the sun climbed higher a certain dinginess appeared here and there in the brighter quarters about them.

"Sleep well?"

"Yes. Yourself?"

Pol nodded.

"But I—"

Mouseglove's eyes shifted sharply to his left and he nodded in that direction. Pol leaned back in his chair and stretched, rolling his head as he did so.

The man who was approaching down the narrow street was clad in black and red as he had been the previous evening. He was looking in their direction.

Pol leaned forward and raised his mug of tea.

"You still can't recall . . . ?" he asked.

Mouseglove shook his head.

"But he's coming this way," he muttered without moving his lips.

Pol took a sip and listened for footfalls. The man had a very soft tread and was almost beside him before he heard a sound.

"Good morning," he said, moving into view. "You are the one called Madwand, of Ibal's company?"

Pol lowered the mug and raised his eyes.

"I am."

"Good." The other smiled. "My name is Larick. I have been appointed to conduct the candidates for initiation to the entrance on the western height of Belken this afternoon. I will also be your guide through the mountain tonight."

"The initiation is to be tonight? I'd thought it was not held until near the end of things?"

"Normally, that is the case," Larick replied, "but I had not been reading my ephemeris recently. I only learned last night when I was appointed to this post that there will be a particularly favorable conjunction of planets tonight—whereas things will not be nearly so good later on."

"Would you care for a cup of tea?"

Larick began to shake his head, then eyed the pot.

"Yes, I am thirsty. Thanks."

He drew up a chair while Pol signaled for a fresh pot.

"My friend's name is Mouseglove," Pol said.

The men studied one another and clasped hands.

"Glad."

"The same."

Larick produced a piece of parchment and a writing stick.

"By the way, I do not really have your name, Madwand, for the list of candidates. How are you actually called?"

In instant reaction Pol's mind slid over the present and back to an earlier time.

"Dan," he said, "Chain—son."

"Dan Chainson," Larick repeated, writing it. "You are fourth on my list. I still have six to go."

"I take it that the rescheduling is as much a surprise to all those involved?"

"I'm afraid so. That's why I have to find everyone in a hurry."

The tea arrived and Pol poured.

"We will meet at the Arch of the Blue Bird," Larick said, gesturing. "It is the farthest archway to the west. It is somewhat south of here, also."

Pol nodded.

"I'll find it. But when do we meet?"

"I was hoping we could all get together by noon," he answered. "But that seems unrealistic, the way things are going. Let's say by the time the sun lies midway between noon and sunset."

"All right. Anything special I should bring?"

Larick studied him for a moment.

"How much preparation have you had for this?" he asked.

Pol wondered whether the flush he felt in his cheeks was visible through his magical disguise, scar and all.

"It depends upon what you mean by preparation," he said. "I've had some instruction as to the metaphysical side of things, but I was counting on more time here for learning something of the practical aspects."

"Then you did not—as your nickname implies—serve what might be referred to as a normal apprenticeship?"

"I did not. I know what I know by means of aptitude, practice and some study—on my own."

Larick smiled.

"I see. In other words, you have had as little preparation as one can have had and still be said to have had some preparation."

"I'd say you've put it properly."

Larick took a drink of tea.

"There is some risk, even for those with full training," he said.

"I already know that."

"Well, it is your decision, and I will have time to go over things somewhat during the climb and while we wait for sundown outside the entrance. To answer your first question, though, bring nothing but the clothes you wear, one small loaf of bread and a flask of water. These may be consumed at any time during the journey, up until the actual entry into the mountain. I would suggest you keep most of it until near the end, as we maintain a total fast during the night's progress through Belken."

Larick finished his tea and rose.

"I'll have to be locating the others now," he said. "Thanks for the tea. I'll see you at the Blue Bird Archway."

"A moment," said Mouseglove.

"Yes?"

"At what point on the mountain will you be emerging in the morning?"

"We'll come out of a cave low on the eastern face—this side, that is. You can't see the place from here. If you want to walk along with me I'm going up to a higher level now. I might be able to point it out to you from there."

"Yes, I'll come."

Mouseglove rose. Pol did also.

A flight of tarnished butterflies swept by as they mounted the stair. When Pol rested his hand against an ornamental column, it felt more like the trunk of a tree than cold stone. The huge gems set into walls had lost much of their brilliance in day's hard glare. But Pol smiled, for the impression of beauty still held despite all of this.

They climbed a hill and Larick pointed at the mountain.

"Yes. Over there," he said. "Near the base—that triangular, darkened area. You can see it if you look closely."

"I see it," Mouseglove said.

"Yes," said Pol.

"Very well. Then I must be on my way. I will see you later."

They watched him head off toward a group of buildings to the south.

"I'll be waiting there when you come out," Mouseglove said. "Don't trust anybody while you're inside."

"Why not?"

"I've gotten the impression here and there that Madwands are looked down upon and resented by those who have served regular apprenticeships. I don't know how strong the feelings might be, but there'll be nine of them in there with you. I wouldn't turn my back on them in any dark corridors."

"You might have a point there. I won't give them any opportunities."

"Shall we stroll back and see whether Ibal is receiving company yet?"

"Good idea."

©JUDY KING RIENIETS 81

But Ibal was not yet receiving. Pol left a message that the schedule had been advanced and that he would be leaving that afternoon. Then he returned to his own quarters and stretched out upon his bed, to rest and meditate. He thought over the entire story of his life as he now knew it—the story of the son of a powerful and evil sorcerer, his life preserved in exchange for his heritage as he was exiled to another world, one which knew no magic. He recalled the day of his return, his bitter reception in this world when he was recognized by means of the dragon birthmark upon his right wrist. He remembered his escape, his flight, his discovery of the ruined family seat at Rondoval and all that went with it—his identity, his powers, his control over the savage beasts that slept there. He relived his conflict with his brilliant but warped step-brother, Mark Marakson, in the anomalous center of high technology which that one had resurrected atop Anvil Mountain in the south. He thought of his brief but doomed affair with the village girl Nora, who had never stopped loving Mark. And now . . .

The Seven. The peculiar manipulation of his life by the seven statuettes, which seemed to have ended that day atop Anvil Mountain, returned to plague his thoughts. He still had no notion as to their true functions, purposes, aims. He felt that he would never enjoy full freedom from apprehension until he came to terms with them. And then the recent unexplained attempt upon his life, and the midnight encounter with the sorcerer who seemed to have answers but did not care to share them . . .

About the only personal thing that did not pass through his mind was a consideration of his recurrent dreams. Soon he fell asleep and had another.

He took his loaf and his water flask with him to the Arch of the Blue Bird. Mouseglove accompanied him to that point. Larick and six of the others were already present. The westering sun had encountered a cloudbank and the city took on its evening sheen prematurely. The other candidates were uniformly young and nervous; and Pol forgot their names—except for Nupf, with whom he was already acquainted.

The sky continued to darken while they waited for the others, and Pol idly let his vision slip into the second seeing. As he cast his gaze about he noted a blue-white pyramid or cone near the center of town, a thing which had not registered itself upon his normal perceptions. Continuing to watch it for a time, he gained the impression that it was growing. He moved his seeing back to its normal mode and the phenomenon faded.

Making his way past the other candidates, he approached Larick who stood, obviously impatient now, watching the massing clouds.

"Larick?"

"What do you want?"

"Just curious. Would you know what that big cone of blue light growing up over there is?"

Larick turned and stared for several moments, then, "Oh," he said. "That is for our benefit—and it reminds me again just how late things are getting. Where the devil are the rest of them?" He turned, looking in several directions, and then a certain tension seemed to go out of him. "Here they come," he said, noting three figures on a distant walkway.

He turned back to Pol.

"That cone you see is the force being raised by an entire circle of sorcerers," he explained. "By the time we enter Belken, it will have reached the mountain and filled it, attuning all ten stations within to greater cosmic forces. As you move from one to the other, each a symbolic representation of one of your own lights, the energies will flow through you and you will thereby be shaped, reshaped and attuned yourself."

"I see."

"I am not certain that you do, Dan. The other nine candidates, serving proper apprenticeships, should have developed their lights properly, in the natural order. For them, tonight's experience should only be an intensification with some minor balancing. With you, though—a Madwand may take any path. It could prove painful, distressing, even maddening or fatal. I do not say this to discourage or frighten, merely to prepare you. Try not to allow anything that occurs to cause you undue distress."

Here Larick bit his lip and looked away.

"Where—where are you from?" he asked.

"A very distant land. I'm sure you would never have heard of it."

"What did you do there?"

"Many things. I suppose I was best at being a musician."

"What about magic?"

"It was not known in that place."

Larick shook his head.

"How could that be?"

"It is just the way that things were."

"Then yourself? How did you come to this land? And how did you become a Madwand?"

For a moment, Pol found himself wanting to tell Larick his story. But prudence put a limit to his desire.

"It is a very long tale," he said, looking back over his shoulder, "and the other three are almost here."

Larick glanced in that direction.

"I suppose that you had some interesting experiences once you discovered your abilities?" he said hurriedly.

"Yes, many," Pol replied. "They might fill a book."

"Do any stand out in your memory as particularly significant?"

"No."

"I get the impression that you do not like to talk about these things. All right. There is no requirement that you do so. But if you would tell me, I would like to know one thing."

"What is that?"

"A white magician may on occasion use what is known as black magic, and vice-versa. We know that it is all much the same and that it is intent that makes the difference—and that it is from intent alone that the magician's path might be described. Have you yet chosen one path or the other?"

"I have used what I had to use as I had to use it," Pol said. "I like to think that my intentions were relatively pure, but then most people so justify themselves in their own eyes. I mean well, most of the time."

Larick smiled and shook his head.

"I wish that I had more time to talk with you, for I feel something very peculiar behind your words. Have you ever used magic with great force against another human being?"

"Yes."

"What became of that person?"

"He is dead."

"Was he also a sorcerer?"

"Not exactly."

" 'Not exactly'? How can that be? A person either is or is not."

"This was a very special case."

Larick sighed and then smiled again.

"Then you are a black magician."

"You said it. I didn't."

The three final candidates now approached the group and were introduced. Larick looked them all over and then addressed them:

"We are late getting started. We will head along this way immediately and then proceed until we have departed the city. The trail
will commence shortly thereafter and we will begin our climb. I do
not know yet how many—if any—rest stops we may make along
the way. It depends on our progress and the time." He gestured
toward a heap of folded white garments. "Each of you pick up a
robe on the way by. We'll don them right before we enter."

He turned and passed under the arch, moving away.

Mouseglove approached Pol.

"I'll be at the exit point in the morning," he said. "Good luck."

"Thanks."

Pol hurried after the others, moving toward the head of the
group. When he glanced back, Mouseglove was gone. He continued his pace until he caught up with Larick, falling into step beside him.

"I am curious," he said, "why you are trying so hard to make
me out a black magician."

"It is nothing to me," the other replied. "Those of all persua-
sions meet and mix freely in this place."

"But I am not. At least, I don't think I am."

"It is of no importance."

Pol shrugged.

"Have it your way, then."

He slowed his pace and fell back among the group of apprentices. Nupf came up next to him.

"Bit of a surprise here, eh?" the apprentice said.

"What do you mean?"

"The suddenness of it all. Ibal doesn't even know I'm on my
way. He's still—" He paused and grinned. "—occupied."

"At least he got my name onto the list before he turned his attention to other matters."

"It was not entirely altruistic of him," Nupf replied. "I envy
you considerably, should you come through this intact."

"How so?"

"You don't know?"

Pol shook his head.

"Madwands—particularly those who make it through initiation," Nupf explained, "are, almost without exception, the most
powerful sorcerers of all. Of course, there aren't that many
around. Still, that is why Ibal would like to have you remember
him with a certain fondness and gratitude."

"I'll be damned," Pol said.

"You really didn't know?"

"Not in the least. Could that have anything to do, I wonder, with Larick's efforts to find out whether I'm black or white?"

Nupf laughed.

"I suppose he hates to see the opposite side get a good recruit."

"What do you mean?"

"Oh, I don't really know that much about him, but the rumor going around among the other candidates has it that Larick is so lily white he spends all of his free time hating the other side. He is also supposed to be very good—in a purely technical sense."

"I'm getting tired of being misjudged," Pol said. "It's been going on all my life."

"It would be best to put up with a little more of it, for now."

"I wasn't thinking of disturbing the initiation."

"I'm sure he'll run it perfectly. Whites are very conscientious."

Pol laughed. He adjusted his vision and looked back at the cone of power. It had grown noticeably. He turned away and moved on toward the mounting clouds. Belken had already acquired something of radiance beneath them.

VI.

Seated upon the wide ledge outside the cavemouth, three-quarters of the way up the mountain's western face, Pol finished his bread and drank the rest of his water while watching the sun sink beneath the weight of starless night. There had been only one brief break on the way up and his feet throbbed slightly. He imagined the others were also somewhat footsore.

There came a flash of lightning in the southwest. A cold wind which had followed them more than halfway up made a little whistling noise among rocky prominences overhead. The mountain had a faint glow to it, which it seemed to acquire every night, only tonight it continued to brighten even as he watched. And when he shifted over to second seeing it seemed as if all of Belken were afire with a slowly undulating blue flame. He was about to comment upon it to Nupf when Larick rose to his feet and cleared his throat.

"All right. Put the robes on over your clothes and line up before the entrance," he said. "It will be a bit of a walk to the first station. I will lead the way. There is to be no talking unless you are called upon for responses."

They unfolded the coarse white garments and began donning them.

". . . And any visions or transformations you may witness—along with any alterations of awareness—are occasions neither for distress nor comment. Accept everything that comes to you, whether it seems good or bad. Transformations themselves may well be transformed before the night is over."

They lined up behind him.

"This is your last chance for questions."

There were none.

"Very well."

Larick proceeded at a deliberate pace into the cavemouth. Pol found himself near the middle of the line which followed him. His vision slipped back into its natural range. The bluish glow di-

minished somewhat but did not depart. The narrow, high-walled
cave into which they entered pulsated in the same fashion as the
outer slopes of the mountain, giving sufficient, if somewhat unsettling, illumination to light their progress. As they passed further
along, the brightness and movement intensified to the point where
the walls were submerged within it, vanishing from sight, and it
was as if they walked a fire-girt avenue out of dream between ce-
lestial and infernal abodes, its direction being a matter of conjec-
ture as well as mood.

A distant rumble of thunder reached them as the way curved to
the left, then to the right, slanting upward. It steepened rapidly
after that, and in a few step-like places the worn floor seemed to
show evidence of human handiwork.

Another turn and it steepened even more sharply, and heavy
guide-ropes appeared at either hand. At first, the candidates were
loath to take hold of them, for the action was tantamount to
placing one's hands among leaping flames; but after a time they
had no choice. There was no sensation of warmth; Pol felt only a
vague tingling on his palms, though his dragonmark began to
throb beneath its disguise after several moments. The air grew
warmer as they mounted, and he could hear the sounds of his
companions' labored breathing as they hurried to keep up with
Larick.

Abruptly, they entered a grotto. The guide-ropes ended. The
floor of the landing on which they halted was more nearly level.
Immediately before them lay a large, circular pool blazing with
white light as if illuminated from below. Low-dipping stalactites
shone like icicles above it. The walls came down almost to its
edges, save for the stony tongue on which they stood. Almost, for
a narrow ledge seemed to circle that entire bright lens of still
liquid.

Larick motioned them out upon the ledge immediately. They
edged their way out and around, backs brushing against the rough
rock. After several minutes, Larick began signing them to halt or
move on, until all of them were distributed in accordance with
some plan known only to himself. Then he moved out to the edge
of the spit from which he had conducted the arrangement and
stared down into the radiant waters. The candidates did the same.

The light dazzled Pol's eyes at first, but he soon became aware
of his own bleached reflection, the irregular sculpture of the roof
like some fantastic landscape behind it. He looked into his own

eyes; a stranger, for this was the face of the disguise he still wore—heavier brow, scar upon the left cheek.

Suddenly, his reflection melted, to be replaced by the image of his true face—leaner, thinner of lip, possessed of a higher hairline—with the white streak running back through his dark locks. He tried to raise his hand to his face and discovered that a strange lethargy with a dull species of sluggishness had come over him. His hand only twitched slightly and he made no further effort to move it. Then he became aware of a voice speaking the words he had but recently learned. It was Larick's, and when he had finished speaking they were repeated by the first candidate upon the far edge of the pool. They echoed through the chamber and tolled inside his head. A faint, sweet scent rose to his nostrils. The next candidate began speaking the same words, and in a part of his mind Pol knew that when his turn came he would be repeating them. Yet, in a way, it seemed as if something within him were already saying them. He felt himself in some way detached from time. There was no time here, only the light and the reflected face. The words rolled toward him, awakening things deep within his being. Then he saw that the reflection was smiling. He was not aware of any movement of his own face. As he watched now, the image wavered and divided itself. It was suddenly as if he had two heads—one which continued smiling to the point of a sneer, the other bearing a massively sad expression. Slowly, they turned to face one another. He was riven by peculiar emotions. How long these persisted, he could not tell, as he observed the two who were one in their archetypal debate. It was only slowly that a vague feeling of wrongness began to come over him.

Then he realized that he was indeed speaking. His turn had come and he had begun his part in the circle without being aware of it. The words vibrated within him, and the world seemed oddly altered—distanced—about him. The light from below his feet grew even brighter. The images within the pool were warped, folded back upon themselves. The two heads of his reflection merged, to become his solitary, unsmiling countenance. A feeling of exhilaration grew within him now and the sense of wrongness was swept away. His head seemed full of light as he uttered the final syllable.

It passed then to the woman to his left, who began the intonation. Pol lost all sense of self now, as well as time and place, and merely existed within the sound and the light, feeling changes pass through him, until it was over.

Without any word or visible sign, he knew when they were

finished. The light in the depths coalesced, seemed to take on the form of a great egg, while the final speaker went through his part. Then, for a long while they stood in silence regarding the depths. Without cue, Pol suddenly raised his head and looked toward Larick. As his gaze moved across the chamber, he saw that all of the others were looking up and turning simultaneously. Slowly then, the candidates moved on along the ledge.

When they reached its end and came onto the pier, Larick raised an arm, gesturing toward his left, then turned and led them through a very narrow cut behind a screen of rock which none had noticed before. After several paces, moving sideways, it widened. Almost immediately, Larick dropped to his hands and knees and crawled into a small, black hole. One by one, the others did the same. The pale, flame-like light and the undulance were present there, also, but inches away in any direction.

Progress was slow, for they worked their way downward, fighting against slippage, crawling flat-bellied through particularly low places, twisting and scraping themselves as they negotiated turns.

The candidate before and below him halted suddenly, and Pol did the same. He heard a grunt from the rear as the one behind him was drawn up short. The walls had paled somewhat to a grayish tone with a pink cast to them.

The candidate before him began inching forward again and Pol did the same, slowly. This continued for approximately one body-length, then was followed by another halt. Pol, still giddy from the opening experience, felt unable completely to control his thoughts. He alternated between mild distress and resignation over this.

After a brief pause, they advanced again, a similar distance. Several more such, and Pol saw its cause. There was a circular opening in the floor. The candidates eased themselves down through it, hung at arm's length and then dropped.

He waited for a time after the one before him passed through, then lowered himself, hung a moment and let go.

It was not a long drop. He landed with his knees bent and immediately moved to the side. Shortly, he joined the others, who stood near the center of the chamber where the roof was high, arranged in a circle in accordance with Larick's gesturing, around the most prominent object in sight—a pink stalactite several times his own height, rising from a large, bumpy, roughly rectangular piece of rock.

When they were all in position about it, Larick motioned them back, spreading the formation to positions as far away from the towering object as the geometry of the cavern permitted. For a moment, the man's eyes met his own, and Pol, unaccountably, felt that there was pain within them. Then Larick moved away, to mount a rock at the far corner of the chamber. Shortly, everyone's gaze left him and returned to the object before them.

Pol relaxed, assuming a contemplative state of mind once again. He looked up and then down the monolith. He felt the power in the place. He slipped his vision into the second seeing for a moment, but there was no change other than an increased brightness to the stalactite. There were not even any drifting strands in the vicinity, a phenomenon which struck him as somewhat odd when he thought about it much later.

At the first slow words from Larick he returned his sight to normal, feeling only the physical sensations which the sounds and their echoes stirred within him. The experiences of timelessness and distancing came over him more quickly than they had on the previous occasion. Now, as he watched, the light on the surface of the towering formation began shifting. It seemed almost as if the thing were moving slightly.

Larick grew silent and some member of the circle began the intonation. The cavern slowly faded about him as this occurred. Pol felt that the huge form was the only tangible object in existence. The words followed him, however, filling this version of the universe which he now occupied. Then, suddenly, the monolith seemed larger, its shape indefinably altered.

Another voice took up the words. Pol watched, fascinated, as the object moved and shifted its appearance. The lumpy base seemed more and more to be the knuckles of three folded fingers, the single upright a forefinger extended, a small, low prominence on its other side the joint of a bent thumb. Of course . . . It had been a hand all along. Why hadn't he noticed sooner?

The voice moved nearer. The hand was indeed stirring, turning in his direction. The finger began to dip, slowly.

His breathing ceased and a sense of awe came over him as it continued to descend toward him. The narrowing distance between them was filled with power. Unaccountably, his right shoulder and arm began to tingle.

The finger, large enough to crush him, reached—gently, delicately—and brushed very lightly against his right shoulder.

He almost collapsed, not from any weight but from the feelings which invaded him at that moment. He steadied himself as the source of the words came even nearer. The finger was retreating now, moving back toward its upright position.

The tingling continued in his arm and shoulder, to be succeeded first by a dull ache and then by a numbness when it came his turn to speak the words. The cavern returned, however, and the hand became once again a stalactite upon a rough rock.

The words went full circle, they meditated in silence for a spell and Larick then motioned them to follow him through an opening in the wall behind the rock upon which he stood.

Pol moved slowly, awkwardly, puzzled by the dead weight which hung at his right side. He reached across and seized his right biceps with his left hand.

His upper arm felt swollen, immense; it was tight against the cloth of his sleeve.

He ran his hand down his arm. The entire limb seemed suddenly grown oversize. Also, it was uniformly diminished in sensitivity. With great effort, however, he found that he could move it. When he lowered his eyes, he discovered that his hand—still normal in appearance and feeling—hung far lower than usual, in the vicinity of his knee. He felt for the power of his dragonmark, but it, too, seemed to have been numbed. Then he recalled Larick's words on the matter of transformations this night—that they should be accepted without distress and not be permitted to interfere with the business at hand. Nevertheless, he glanced surreptitiously at the others, to see whether he could detect any malformations. The few he was able to view before entering the tunnel did not exhibit any gross impairments. And no one seemed to notice his own.

They walked. The way was level, straight and sufficiently wide. The illumination persisted. They passed through an empty chamber without halting—where it seemed that a high-pitched musical tone was being constantly sounded, just beyond the bounds of audibility—and they continued until another grotto opened before them.

Here they entered. It was a rounded chamber with a curved roof, almost bubble-like in appearance. Larick spaced them about a rock formation resembling a cauldron, near its center. Again, a chanting commenced and again Pol knew the oceanic feeling, the detachment he had experienced at the other stations, though here it was mixed with something of depression, sadness. His left arm acquired the tingling sensation at this point, and when his turn had come and passed and all was done it resembled the right exactly in its transformation.

This time he accepted the change with less distress, as part of the total experience. The others must be undergoing similar experiences, he decided. He followed them to a well-like depression across the way, discovering as he did that sensation, mobility and control were returning to his arms.

He watched the others. A knotted rope fastened about a nearby rock hung down into the hole. One by one, the candidates took hold and climbed down it, vanishing into the darkness. When his turn came he did likewise, with great ease, pleased with the enormous strength which now resided in his arms and shoulders.

In the yellow-blue cavern to which they descended the now-familiar ritual formation was established and the rite carried out about a large, spherical crystal set upon a pedestal. Before it was concluded, Pol's left hand felt as if he had dipped it in boiling water. He gave no outward evidence of this, not even looking down upon it, until after this phase, too, was completed and Larick led them out through an opening in the wall to the left.

The hand still throbbed, but the sensation of heat had vanished. When he viewed it, he saw that it had grown massive, purplish, scaly; the nails were thick, dark, triangular, hooked, at the ends of long, powerful-looking digits which reached almost to his ankle. The robe he wore concealed much of the change within its folds, its long, wide sleeves. Still . . . He looked about again. None of the other candidates seemed to have noticed his discomfort. Again, he forced the thought of it away. He trekked after the others along a broad, level tunnel, his gait somewhat disturbed, as if by overbalancing and compensation.

A sword hung from a chain midway between floor and roof at the near end of the next chamber. This, in its turn, became the object of their meditation, swinging and glinting redly as the words circled it. The visions which swam through his mind at this, as at the previous station, barely registered themselves on his consciousness, as the feeling of the power of his new limbs came to occupy his awareness with the burning pang in his right hand—this time a thing of masochistic pleasure to him. He spoke the words in a ringing voice and did not even look down, already knowing what he would see.

When it was over, he turned and joined the line filing out through another opening and into a downward-slanting tunnel, moving now as if within a dream, his actions determined by some a-logical pattern he could feel about him, no longer wondering whether the others' notions of personal transformation coincided with his own.

The way was steep; sweet odors rose up it. The walls were a living net of pale fire. The floor sparkled, almost moistly. They continued downward for a long while, coming at last to a small chamber into which they were crowded about a simple, unadorned cube of stone. The place was strewn with flowers, accounting for the odor he had detected on the way down. Here he found the smell almost sickly sweet in its intensity. When the words were spoken in these close quarters they hurt his ears. He felt excessively warm and became very conscious of the beating of his heart. A wave of dizziness passed over him, but he knew that even if he fainted there was no place to fall, so closely were they packed together. Later, he believed that he had actually succumbed to unconsciousness briefly, for there was a gap in his memory up until he found himself speaking. It seemed that there had been another vision, one which had partly numbed his senses. He could not recall the details. His heart was beating rapidly now, with an unusually heavy throbbing. He became peripherally aware that the candidates who stood at either hand were removed a greater distance from him than they had been the last time he had been aware of their presence. The aroma of the flowers had diminished sharply, or else he had become accustomed to it.

He lowered his head as he finished speaking and saw that his robe was torn. Then he became aware of the enormous breadth of his shoulders, the barrel-like girth of his chest. No wonder his garment was rent. How could this be an illusion? He glanced at the nearest candidates. Wrapped in their own meditations, none of them seemed to be paying him any heed.

Slowly, he raised his right hand. He reached inside through the torn place, groped about until he located an opening in his own garments which lay beneath. His heavy fingers explored below them, encountering a tough, hard, bumpy surface. He explored further. From navel to neck, it felt as if he were covered with scales. He withdrew his hand and let it fall. When he looked up again, he saw that Larick was staring at him. The man looked away immediately.

When they departed the room, it was as if they followed a continuation of the tunnel which had brought them to that place, still slanting downward, headed in the same direction. He controlled

his breathing carefully as they walked, for its sounds came heavy
and stertorous when he drew deep breaths.

There came a cooling for which he was grateful, as they continued down the long shaft. The next chamber was much larger than
the one they had quitted, its floor of a greenish stone. A heavy oil
lamp was suspended by chains from its roof, and its flames waved
as the words were spoken.

This time it was his left leg. The moment that the tingling began
he knew what was to follow. When it finally came, he almost
collapsed. The leg seemed to have grown much longer and heavier
than the right one. He was almost completely unbalanced and had
to keep that knee bent and the other straight. But, if anything, the
dream quality he was experiencing was enhanced by this phase of
the ritual progress. As they turned and he lurched his way along a
mercifully level tunnel, visions, like objectified free associations,
were everywhere. He could not place his hand against the swimming wall for support without seeming to touch some beast-face
or a woman's breast, a flower or the feathers of a bird.

In this frame of mind, he was not even certain what he saw in
the next chamber. That it was large and scented, he was aware. The
images seemed everywhere dense. Zodiacal beasts moved in procession before him. If he fixed his eyes upon one, it dissolved into
an entirely new series of forms. After a time, he gave up. He almost welcomed the tightening and the warmth in his right leg
when it came, for his balance was finally restored when that one
matched the other.

His mind a chaotic jumble now, he departed with the others,
moving surely and swiftly down another long, steep way.

They came at last into a very dark chamber where stalactite and
stalagmite were joined to form a towering silver pillar about which
Larick led and placed them. Pol's mind cleared momentarily, and
he wondered what had actually been happening and for how long
the ceremony had been going on. The images were dispersed.
There was only the shining pillar here, lovely and bright. With his
elongated reach, he felt that he could almost extend his arms and
embrace it. The thing seemed to reflect power. He felt some sort
of stability returning. He raised his massive hands and stared at
them. Where had he seen their like before? He adjusted his vision
for the second sight, but they remained unchanged when this occurred.

He let his hands fall as the memory came to him. They were
like the hands of those demonic creatures he had seen in his

© JUDY KING RIENIETS

dreams of the land beyond the Gate. What could this mean? Why were they being objectified in this fashion during this ritual of a supposedly beneficial nature? Was this truly the sort of transformation of which Larick had spoken, or was he undergoing something else?

He raised a hand to his face, ran his fingertips across his features. They seemed unchanged, yet—

He was seized by an abdominal cramp which bent him partway forward. Involuntarily, he clutched at his midsection. In that instant, Larick began speaking again, yet another sequence of the words. He felt the pressure of his belt and unfastened it. He heard the sound of cloth tearing beneath his robe. When the pains had passed, he was aware of a widening in the pelvic area, a spreading of his hips. It was difficult when he attempted to stand fully upright. His spine now seemed to possess a curvature which bore him forward so that his hands rested upon the ground. His feet began to ache.

Then it did not matter. The moment of full rationality passed, and he was caught up in another sequence of visions and feelings of power. It seemed that a very long time had passed. His mind drifted through the repetitions and his own part in them. When they moved again, he followed, slouched far forward, oblivious and ignored.

Larick led them to an opening in the floor through which the top of a ladder protruded. He motioned for them to follow after and proceeded to descend it.

Pol waited until all of the others had gone down before beginning his own clumsy descent.

The ladder creaked beneath him and one rung came loose. But he clutched its sides tightly and kept going. It was a long descent, finally taking him directly into the midst of the others, who stood within a circle drawn upon the floor of this chamber. He noted that two of the other candidates had collapsed and that Larick was kneeling, massaging the chest of one of them.

He jumped down the final few feet and waited. The man on whom Larick had been working moaned after a time and sat up. Larick immediately moved to the other—a small, red-haired man, whose teeth seemed tightly locked together—and listened for a heartbeat. Apparently there was none, for he abandoned that one immediately and returned to the other. After several minutes, he helped that other to his feet and checked the red-haired man again. The second form remained still. Larick shook his head and rose, leaving the man where he had fallen. He motioned the others into a formation around himself, then raised both hands.

Pol's feet began to ache as the power was raised within the circle. The pain grew so severe that he had to tear off his boots seconds later. He held them beneath his arm inside the robe as the ritual progressed. He dimly recalled that this was the final stage of the initiation. Everything would be over soon and he could go somewhere and sleep . . .

He found himself saying the words, his voice normal, steady. When he had finished, he closed his eyes. An extraordinarily vivid image immediately arose. He saw Rondoval besieged, a storm raging about it. The image flowed. A man stood upon the main balcony, a black scarf about his neck, the scepter of power in hands. His hair was frost-white save for a black streak running back through it. He was singing orders to his unearthly hordes and causing flames to rise before his enemies. But a sorcerer all in white—old Mor!—came to duel with him. The older man prevailed, the defense slackened, the man on the balcony slumped and withdrew.

Inside, he raced to a nearby chamber and began manipulating magical paraphernalia. The action was telescoped. Moments later, it seemed, scepter held high, he stood at the Circle's center, voicing words of power that rang through the room, causing a twisting, smoky shape in a corner near the ceiling to vibrate in resonance.

"Belphanior ned septut!" he cried. "Bel—"

The door burst open and a messenger entered and collapsed as the forces swept over him.

"The gate has been breached . . ." he said, before he expired.

The sorcerer spoke a word of protection, thrust the scepter into his sash and broke the Circle.

He departed the chamber, raced up the hall and entered another room, where he seized and braced a powerful bow which hung there. He chose a single arrow from a soft leather quiver and took it with him.

Below, Pol saw him use the weapon to slay the leader of the attacking forces. Then he fought a duel with old Mor, was bested and died, buried beneath a heap of rubble.

Things blurred. The storm had passed. The fighting had ceased. He saw Mor mounted upon the back of a centaur, riding into the west, the dead sorcerer's body tied across the back of another of the horse-people.

Another blur.

Within a cavern, illuminated by his glowing staff, planted like some unnatural tree, Mor was alone with the dead sorcerer. The body was laid on its back upon a slab of stone, arms folded. Leaning above the corpse, Mor was doing something to the face—rubbing, pressing. At some later point he raised his hands and seemed to pull the face away.

No. It was a deathmask that he held upraised, and in that moment Pol noticed how closely the features resembled those of Mor himself.

He began speaking softly, but Pol could not distinguish the words. The second seeing came over him and he beheld a fine, silver strand attached to the mask.

Everything came apart and trailed away then, as visions do.

Pol opened his eyes. Everyone was standing in meditation and there was an echoing sound in the air, Larick's hands were raised and he was clapping them together slowly, speaking certain final words.

When he had finished, Larick passed among them, stopped and raised the dead man, positioned him across his back, moved to its perimeter and broke the Circle. He turned then and gestured for the others to follow him.

They exited the chamber and moved along a widening tunnel, passing at length into a large, irregularly shaped, unadorned cavern cluttered with rock and stalagmite, hung with huge stalactites. The air there was cooler still. Pol's head began to clear.

Larick picked his way across the cavern and found a place to deposit the body. Then he returned, mounted a small prominence and addressed his followers:

"Krendel was the only candidate who succumbed to the forces," he said. "The rest of you may be said to have passed, in one fashion or another. It could be several weeks before the new alignment of your magical states has stabilized. Because of this, I caution you against any operations of the Art for a time. Things could go very much awry, with unpredictable results. Wait, rest, confine your activities to the physical plane. When you feel ready, begin your workings in a very small way—and wait after each step, to be certain that things are proceeding properly."

He turned and looked back over his shoulder. He gestured in that direction.

"That tunnel leads back into the world," he said. "It is long. I will conduct each of you up it personally, to meet the dawn."

"You will be first," he told the nearest. "Go and wait for me over there. I will join you in a moment."

He stepped down from the mound and headed toward Pol.

"Come over here," he whispered, and he led him into a side passage behind a fat stalagmite.

"Something is wrong," Pol said. "I've become a monster and no one seems to notice."

"That is true," Larick answered, raising his voice to a normal pitch.

"Should this not pass, now the initiation is over?"

"Madwand," he replied, "your transformation had nothing to do with the initiation. Can you say you know nothing of the House of Avinconet?"

"Yes. I've never heard of it."

"Nor of the great Gate to a dark and sinister world? A Gate you would fling wide?"

Pol frowned.

"I see," Larick said, sighing. "What I did to you was indeed necessary. I took the opportunity afforded by your state of mind at each stage of the initiation to lay powerful spells upon you—exchanging your body, piece by piece, for that of one of the dwellers in that accursed place. Save, of course, for your head."

"Why?" Pol asked. "What have I done to you?"

"Personally, nothing," Larick answered. "But the evil you would work is so great that everything I have done is warranted. You will learn more of what lies before you by and by. Now I must get back to the other initiates."

Pol extended one massive, taloned hand to seize him. Larick gestured briefly and the entire limb was instantly paralyzed.

"What—?"

"I have complete control of your new body," the other stated. "I have enfolded you in a series of virtually unbreakable spells. See how I lay my will upon you, totally immobilizing you now? There is also a masking spell. It even compensates for your ungainliness. Only you see yourself as you truly are—a necessary reminder, I'd say. You are now, in all ways, my creature."

"And you were so concerned about black magic," Pol said. "Perhaps you feared competition?"

Larick winced and looked away.

"It was necessary, this time," he said, "to combat a greater ill."

"Don't preach me that line. I've done nothing wrong. You have."

Larick turned away. Pol screamed at him.

His cry was cut short as the man turned back and gestured again. Now Pol could no longer speak at all.

"I'll come for you last and we will journey to Castle Avinconet," Larick said, and then he smiled. "Don't go away."

He passed the rocky corner and was gone.

Pol heard a drop of water fall from a stalactite into a nearby pool. He heard the sounds of his own shallow breathing. He heard the distant voices of the other initiates, doubtless discussing the night's experiences.

If magic had bound him, then magic could free him, he decided. But he could not locate the sources of his own power. It seemed as if that part of him were somehow asleep. He brooded over Larick's words, over the fact that his dreams were apparently a nasty reality to someone else. He sought through his memories for some clue as to why this should be so. He wondered whether his present situation were in any way connected with the attack of the sorcerer Mouseglove had dispatched back at Rondoval. He strained to move, but no movement followed.

Then there came the sound of a footstep beyond the passage. It seemed too soon for Larick to be returning, but—

A large man, as tall but wider than Larick, turned the corner and advanced. His face was a constantly shifting thing, as if seen through a multi-phase refracting medium. The eyes drifted, the nose swelled and shrank, the mouth twisted through ghastly parodies of human expressions. But when he opened it to speak, Pol still saw that there was a shining, capped tooth. He tried the second seeing but was unable to penetrate the distortion spell the person wore like a mask.

"I see that my disguise still holds for your features," came the familiar voice. "But what have you done with the rest?"

Pol found that he could not even snarl.

"Actually," the man went on, "that is a terrific body. You could wreak all sorts of havoc with it, if you'd a mind to. I suppose you're rather attached to your own, though, eh?"

He raised his head, one huge eye and one small one focusing upon Pol's own, shifting relative sizes even as he stared.

"Forgive me," he said then. "I'd forgotten you can't answer."

He raised one hand and slapped Pol lightly across the mouth. It stung for only a moment, and something seemed to be released with the stinging. Pol found that his jaws were unlocked, that he could move his head.

"What the hell is going on?" he asked.

"I haven't the time to tell you, even if I wished to," the other replied. "It's a long story and there are other considerations of much greater moment just now. Everything seems to be coming along nicely, though. I wouldn't worry too much."

"You call this 'nicely'?" Pol said, casting his gaze down over his monstrous form.

"Well, not necessarily from an esthetic standpoint, if you happen to be human," the man said. "I was referring to the progression of events. Larick thinks he's got you now."

"Offhand, I'd say he's right."

"That might be remedied, if you're willing to play the game out."

"I don't even know the stakes, or the rules."

"That will be a part of your reward if all goes well: answers to your questions—and answers to some you haven't even thought of yet."

"Such as who you are, and what you're after?"

"That will almost assuredly come out."

"Will I like what I discover?"

"In matters of taste, each person is of course the only judge."

"What choice have I?"

"You may act, or be acted upon."

"What do you want me to do?"

"Go along with things, find out what it is that your captor desires and decide whether that is what you also want. Then you act accordingly. Larick feels that he has you under complete control, but in a moment I will break his infantile spells. I will also reverse the moderately clever body exchange he has worked upon you, restoring to you your own vigorous, youthful—if fatigued—carcass. Then will follow the work of a true master. Freed and restored, I will disguise your body as I disguised your features, giving to it in every respect the semblance of the monster you now are. For an encore, I will then cloak you in a masking spell in all ways identical to the one which now hides your hideous appearance from most mortal eyes—"

"A disguise within a disguise?"

"Precisely."

"To what end?"

"At some point, those who desire you in the reduced state will be sure to strip away the outer layer to behold the captive monster within."

The large sorcerer strode forward and clasped him by the shoulders. Instantly, Pol felt something like an electric shock pass through him. His arm dropped. He sagged forward. His boots fell to the floor from where he had clutched them beneath his left arm all this long while. The sorcerer seized that arm and an agonizing pain ran through it. Before Pol could examine it, he had hold of the other. He was humming as he worked. Whether or not this was a part of his procedure, Pol could not tell.

As he raised his hands and realized that they were indeed *his* hands again, the man struck him a mighty blow across the back with his left hand and upon the chest just above the heart with his right. Even within the well-muscled and heavily armored form that he wore, Pol could tell that the man was no weakling.

He felt the air rush out of his lungs as his chest cavity was returned to normal. He began to straighten and the sorcerer struck him a terrific blow in the abdomen, well below the belt. The change continued in that region, and he straightened fully, massaging, slapping himself, as much for the joy of feeling his own form again as to ease the omnipresent aches.

The big sorcerer kicked him in the shins and he felt the aches, straightening and shrinkage begin in his legs.

"I must say you have a violent approach to these matters," he remarked.

"Perhaps you'd prefer a six-hour incantation with incense?"

"I never argue with success."

"Prudent. I now begin the first masking spell, causing you to look as you just were."

The illusion began, growing like a gray mist about him, shaped by the flowing gestures of the face-changer's hands. Pol felt his hidden dragonmark throb in the presence of this magic. Soon it cloaked him completely, coalescing, sinking through his garments.

The sorcerer sighed and straightened.

". . . And that will be all they see, if they pierce your outer guise, soon to be supplied by me. I must caution you concerning the obvious, however."

"That being?"

"You must act as if you are still under control. Be standing paralyzed in the same position in which he left you when Larick returns. Follow all of his orders as if you had no choice. The moment you deviate, you lose your chance to learn anything further. You will probably also have a fight on your hands."

Pol nodded. He looked down at himself as he did, seeing the monstrous appearance once again but not feeling it.

"I'll mask this illusion for everyone else now, as Larick had it," the sorcerer said, "but leave the appearance for you, as he also had it, as a reminder to act in keeping with it—with clumsiness and obedience."

Pol watched the man's hands as they commenced an intricate series of gestures.

"Do you see strands when you work?" he asked him suddenly.

"Sometimes," the sorcerer replied. "But right now I see beams of colored light, which I intercept. Hush. I'm concentrating."

Pol fixed his eyes on the man's changing face, trying to guess at his true features. But there was no pattern to the changes.

When the movements ceased and the man straightened, Pol said, "You told me on that night you came to me in our camp that our interests might not be entirely conjoined."

"Oh, there is a possibility that we might wind up at odds," the other replied. "I hope not, but there you are. It could happen. If so, it won't be because I didn't try, though. And at least for the moment we want the same thing: to get you out of here intact, to deceive your enemies, to position you strategically."

"Have you any idea what will happen when I leave here?"

"Oh, yes. You will be spirited away almost immediately—to Castle Avinconet."

"Larick did say that much. But who else is involved. And what will I meet at that end?"

"It is far better for you to learn these things yourself, to keep your responses normal."

"Damn it! There's more to it than that! You're hiding something!"

"In what way does that make me different from other men? Play your part, boy. Play your part."

"Don't patronize me. I need more information to carry this thing off."

"Bullshit," the sorcerer replied and turned away. "And strike your pose again. I believe I hear someone coming."

"But—"

"The rest is silence," the changing man said, as he vanished around the corner.

VII.

Mouseglove hunkered in a rocky recess to the left of the cave-mouth, his hood raised and cloak drawn about him against the morning's chill. To his right, the fresh-risen sun constructed morning above the foothills, skimming a layer of glory from the magical city he had quitted hours before. Eight of the initiates had so far passed him, each in the company of Larick, to salute the dawn, then make their ways back toward the town, alone, or in the company of a servant or former master. When he heard footsteps once again, Mouseglove stirred slightly, turning his head toward the opening. When he saw Pol approaching with the leader, he rose, joints creaking, but did not immediately depart his station.

Unlike those who had preceded him, Pol had already removed his white robe. His gait was slower and more awkward than usual. Larick, too, was dressed only in his day garments and head cloth. His face bore a far less solemn aspect than it had when he was bringing the others forth from Belken. He was snapping orders at Pol as they emerged. The two immediately turned to their left and began walking quickly in that direction.

Puzzled, Mouseglove stepped out from his niche and hurried after them.

"Good morning," he said. "How did you fare during the night?"

Larick almost stumbled in halting, and he placed his hand upon Pol's arm. By the time he turned, his face was composed. Pol, moving more slowly, was without expression.

"Good morning," Larick replied. "Your friend is well enough physically, but some who go through initiation experience mental disorganization in varying degrees. This has occurred with him."

"How serious is this thing?"

"That depends upon a great many factors—but it is generally treatable. I was hurrying him off right now with that end in mind."

"That is why you skipped the dawn salutation?"

Larick's eyes narrowed for the briefest moment, as if assessing the other's knowledge of the matters involved.

"We were not going to dispense with it entirely," he said. "But perhaps you are right, since this is the traditional spot."

He turned toward the place where the others had stood to perform the final ritual function.

"Pol! Do you at least understand me?" Mouseglove said.

Larick turned back.

"I am certain that he does," he told him. "But, technically, he should not address anyone until he has finished with this part of things. You can see in a few minutes what his response will be."

He led Pol over to the place, speaking softly and rapidly to him. Mouseglove shifted about, glancing in every direction. A little later, he saw Pol raise his arms and lift his face toward the light in the east. As Pol began to mutter, Larick moved a short distance away from him. Mouseglove watched carefully, hands beneath his cloak.

When Pol had completed a hurried version of the sunrite, he turned toward the smaller man.

"It may not be all that serious," he said then. "But I must go away with Larick for a time. I can afford to take no chances in something like this."

"How long?"

"I do not know. For as long as is necessary."

"It could take a week or two," Larick put in. "Possibly even longer."

"Where is it that you are taking him? I'm going with you."

"I couldn't tell you that until I have conferred with some experts. Perhaps he can be treated here. Then again, he may have to go away."

"Where?"

"That remains to be determined."

"Pol," Mouseglove said, "are you certain that this is what you want to do?"

"Yes," Pol replied.

"Very well. We will go and find out. If it is to be here, I will wait. If it is to be elsewhere, I will accompany you."

"That will not be necessary," Pol said, and he turned away. "I don't need you."

"Nevertheless . . ."

"You are an encumbrance!" Larick said, and he raised his hand.

Mouseglove moved, but not fast enough. All strength and sensation fled his limbs. He fell, his hand still gripping the butt of the pistol he had been unable to draw.

For some time before he opened his eyes, Mouseglove was marginally aware of a slow, intermittent, shuffling sound. When finally he did open them, his field of vision was occupied by a small, gray, mossy rock and a scattering of gravel. He noted that the day had grown perceptibly brighter.

He moved his left hand slowly, placing its palm flat upon the ground near to his shoulder. It remained there for long seconds before he became aware of the coldness of the stone. The shuffling sound came again and he raised his head a few inches, suddenly aware of a stiffness in his neck. He pushed hard with the hand, heaving himself upward, rolling into a seated position, fighting a tendency to slump forward. As his gaze moved across the area, passing the place where Pol and Larick had stood, his memory of the morning's events poured into his mind. He turned his head to the east. The station of the sun told him that an hour or more had passed since that encounter. He rehearsed the entire exchange, seeking clues as to what had occurred within the mountain and what might now be afoot. He resolved that the next time he argued with a sorcerer he would have the weapon drawn and pointed at its target.

A series of small sounds reached him from within the cave, turning itself into several rapid footfalls and then halting. He drew one knee beneath him and pushed himself up into a crouch. He rose slowly as the footfalls came again, nearing the mouth of the cave. He drew the weapon and pointed it at the opening, the hammer making a clicking sound as he set it.

The steps grew stronger, steadier. A moment later, a small, red-haired man appeared within the opening. He was wearing a dirt-streaked white robe. He leaned against the rock, eyes rolling and blinking, head turning. When his gaze swept over Mouseglove, it did not pause. His complexion was dead white. He twitched and jerked, as though he were having a minor seizure.

Mouseglove watched him closely for a long while before he spoke.

"What is the matter?" he asked, weapon still steady.

The head rolled again, the eyes passing over him, then back again, back again, their orbit narrowing, a rapid scanning motion.

At last, they seemed to focus upon him, but the look they held caused him to suppress a shudder.

"What is the matter?" he repeated.

The man took a step forward, raised a pale hand, opened his mouth and inserted the fingers. He made a gargling noise, then withdrew his fingers slightly, pinching the tip of his tongue. He took another step, released the tongue, held both hands at shoulder level. He took another step, and another, his right hand moving from side to side, gradually reaching forward. He continued to make gasping, rattling noises, and his tread grew more steady.

"Hold it!" Mouseglove said. "What do you want?"

The man roared at him and rushed forward.

"Stop!" Mouseglove cried, and when the man did not he pulled the trigger.

The round struck the man in the left arm, turning him sideways. He swayed for a moment, then dropped to his knees, making no effort to reach for the area of impact. He rose again almost immediately, turning back toward Mouseglove, voicing a new series of gutturals.

"Don't make me shoot again," Mouseglove said, setting the hammer. "I recognize you. I know you're one of the candidates. Just tell me what you want."

The man kept coming, and Mouseglove fired again.

The man jerked and was turned sideways again, but this time he did not fall. He straightened and resumed his progress, his steady stream of sounds acquiring more and more inflection.

"Aaalll riight . . ." he said.

Mouseglove licked his lips as he readied the weapon once more. "For gods' sakes, stop!" he cried. "I don't want to do this to you!"

"Not im—por—tant. Listenlistenlistenlisten," the other said, face totally devoid of expression, eyes still rolling, hands still extended and twitching.

Mouseglove backed off three paces, but the other hastened once more, Mouseglove halted then and shot him squarely in the chest.

The man was jolted by the blow. He fell backward, caught himself in a seated position and began to rise again.

"No!" Mouseglove cried. "Please! Stop!"

"Stop," the man repeated without emotion. "Listen, listen, listen. Pol. Im—por—tant. You."

"Pol?" Mouseglove said, cocking the weapon again. "What about him?"

"Yes. Pol. Yes. You un-der-stand—me—now. Yes?"

"Then stay put and tell me! Don't come any nearer!"

Slowly, the other rose again, and something which had registered without Mouseglove's realizing it, came into his consciousness at that moment.

The man was not bleeding from any of his wounds. The garment was torn, darkened, slightly damp-looking where each round had penetrated—but there were no bright red splotches.

"Stay—put?" he said. "Stand—here?"

"Yes. You make me very nervous. I can hear you clearly. Tell me from there. What about Pol?"

"Pol . . ." said the other, swaying. "In trouble, Mouseglove. Listen."

"I am listening. What sort of trouble is it?"

"Larick—placed him—under a spell."

"What sort of spell? I'll find someone who can lift it."

"Not necessary. It has been removed. But Larick—does not—know this."

"Then Pol's mind is all right?"

"As always."

"But Larick thinks he is under a spell?"

"Yes. As Pol wishes."

"Where is he taking him?"

"Castle Avinconet."

"That's Ryle Merson's place! I might have known. I will go there and help him in whatever he is about."

"Not yet. You would be of little help and likely be destroyed. There is a better course of action."

"Name it."

"Go to Pol's patron."

"Ibal?"

"That one. Tell him what has occurred. Ask him for speedy transportation back to Rondoval."

"Say he grants it. What then?"

"You can speak with dragons."

"I'm afraid so."

"Tell the old one—Moonbird—to take you to the dead crater on Anvil Mountain and there help you to recover the magical tool."

"The scepter?"

"Yes."

"Say this can be done."

"Then take it to Pol at Avinconet."

"He will be all right in the meantime?"

"They may see fit to destroy him at any time. I do not know. If they do not, however, he may well need it soon."

"Who are you?"

"I do not know."

"How do you know all these things?"

"I was there."

"Why do you wish to help Pol?"

"I am uncertain."

"How is it that I could not kill you?"

"A corpse cannot die."

"Now it is I who do not understand."

"You know enough. Good-bye."

The red-haired man collapsed and lay still. Mouseglove approached him cautiously. There was no sign of breathing, and he considered the man's waxy pallor at closer range. He reached out and touched a cheek. It was cold. He raised the right hand. It was cold, also; and a certain stiffness had already come into the limb. He pressed upon the fingernails one after the other. They all grew white and remained so. Finally, he leaned forward and lay his ear upon the chest near to the bullet hole. He discovered it to be a quiet place.

He arranged the body, crossing the arms upon the breast. He drew the white cowl up over the head and down across the face. He rose and moved away.

Crossing to the place where Pol and Larick had stood, he located their tracks and began following them. They disappeared quickly, however, in the rocky terrain. He halted there and spent several minutes pondering. Then he turned to the city of illusion and began his descent toward its flickering towers.

VIII.

Wind whistling past him, cloak flapping behind him, Pol leaned forward upon the shoulders of the lesser dragon—a lithe, brown creature of similar mien and considerably less mass than the giant beasts of Rondoval—his legs gripping the sides of its back-ridge, hands upon a leather harness it wore. Twenty meters to his left and a few higher, Larick was similarly mounted upon one of the leathern-winged creatures. He glanced occasionally at Pol, who maintained an impassive attitude. A number of bright strands, visible at the second seeing, ran between them. Pol wondered how difficult it might be to kill the other when the time finally came. He decided that magic was too slow and uncertain a thing when employed against another sorcerer. He decided to strike quickly, with full violence and without warning once he had learned what he needed to know and could afford to dispense with the man. It would be foolhardy to leave enemies of his sort alive.

The sun was about to cut the throat of another day in the west and the moon had long since risen—a pale rag tossed above cloud-crests, brightening now over rough and shadowed land—as north and west they headed, long necks of their dark mounts extended, vanes outstretched and occasionally booming against gusts.

They had changed mounts four times during the day, finding the fresh ones magically tethered at a series of high locales. Pol's shoulder and leg muscles had long before ached themselves to the point of numbness. He stole a glance at Larick, who seemed tireless, bent forward and urging his mount to greater efforts. He stared ahead as if trying to burn holes through the darkening air.

Avinconet, Avinconet . . . He had repeated the name to himself for hours, in time with the rhythms of the flight. He had answered truthfully in telling Larick he had known nothing of it, yet—

It seemed now as if there might be some small familiarity attached. It seemed possible that there had been references in some of his father's earlier journals, though he could not recall anything specific.

Avinconet. Avinconet and Rondoval . . . Had there been some sort of tie?

The sun dipped lower and the moon grew brighter—and then, splashed with daysblood, he saw it, spread across the face of one of the more prominent peaks of a distant range. And he knew that he knew it.

Avinconet was the castle of his dreams, through which he had passed on his way to the Gate. Somehow, he had known all along that it was a real place. But seeing it . . . Seeing it gave rise to a train of disturbing sensations. He found himself anxious to enter the place, to locate the Gate. There was something that he had to do there, wanted to do, despite a reflex squeamishness at the very thought of the Gate. Yet, precisely what that action was, he could not say.

He watched the grim architecture grow before him, paling to yellow, silver, gray-white—a huge, central keep, stepped like a terrace, bristling with towers at many levels, flanked by long ranks of attached side-buildings—surrounded by high, wide ramparts, battlemented, possessed of numerous angles, a squat tower atop each turning. Windows were lighted at several levels toward the right side of the main structure. He shifted to the second seeing and immediately noted a tremendous massing of strands high in the air above the rear of the keep. He also noted a small, pale light drifting along the forward wall from left to right, pausing occasionally, wavering.

When they reached a position above the place, Larick swung his mount into a huge circle and Pol's followed, buffeted by strong winds. They commenced a slow, downward spiral.

As they descended toward the larger of a number of courtyards toward the rear, Pol continued to study the small light, visible only with the second seeing. It appeared human in form from this nearer distance, and there was a long, pale strand attached to it. Something about its aspect at this level touched him with a vague feeling of mournfulness.

As they dropped lower, Pol saw that the rear wall of the enclosed area was rough rock—a part of the mountainside itself—pierced by a number of irregular dark openings, several of them barred. It was at about this point that the light upon the ramparts disappeared from sight.

They touched down roughly and Larick alit at once. Moments

later, Pol felt his strings jerked and he followed him. Larick un-
harnessed the beasts, shouted an order and watched them shuffle
off into one of the cave-like openings. He followed them and drew
upon something in the shadows. A metal grillwork dropped into
place with a clang which echoed through the court.

Larick returned to Pol.

"We made excellent time because of the tailwinds," he commented. "I didn't think we'd be getting in till after midnight. He
might be able to see you now. I don't know. I'll have to check."

"Who is 'he'?" Pol asked.

"Ryle Merson, the master of Avinconet."

"What does he want with me, wizard?"

"That is really for him to tell you. Come this way."

Pol felt a tugging upon the strands Larick had affixed to his
person. He made no resistance but followed their lead toward an
open archway to what he judged the northeast. They passed
through into a flagstoned corridor where Larick led him about a
series of turns.

Left, right, left, left, Pol memorized.

And then they halted before a low doorway. Its heavy wooden
door stood ajar and Larick pushed it the rest of the way open. Pol
noted that it could be secured from the outside by means of a
heavy wooden bar.

"Inside," Larick said, and power pulsed in the strands.

Pol moved forward, stooped and entered. A bench ran along
the righthand wall of the small, low-ceilinged room. There were
no windows, only a few air-slits at the upper corners. A ragged
blanket and a heap of sacking lay upon the bench. There was a
chamber pot upon the floor nearby. An empty candle-bracket was
affixed to the wall above the bench.

Pol turned back after he had passed over the threshold and the
compulsion ceased.

"What's for dinner?" he asked.

"If he can't see you now, I'll have something sent over," Larick
replied.

"I'll study the wine list while I wait."

Larick stared at him, shook his head.

"You could use a few more restraints. I don't want you tearing
this place apart," he said. "Go sit down on the bench."

"All right, wizard. Not much to tear, though."

Pol crossed the room and seated himself. He could feel the
working of the strands about him almost immediately.

"You do that very well," he said.

"Thanks."

". . . But I don't believe it will save you in the end."

Larick chuckled.

". . . So long as the end is a great way off."

"Don't buy any long playing records," Pol said.

"What does that mean?"

"Even if you find out, it will be too late."

"Have it your way, Chainson."

"I may."

The door closed. The room became very dark. Pol heard the bar slide into place. He shook off the restraining strands.

He had toyed with the idea of trying to get a strand onto Larick while Larick was restraining him, a thing which would permit him to follow the other's progress about the place, seeing some of the things which he regarded. He had dismissed the notion as too risky, but now he wondered . . .

When he switched to the second seeing, the room was bathed in a pearly glow. A pale golden strand hovered near the door. He raised his right hand and exerted his will. Beneath multiple layers of illusion his dragonmark throbbed. The filament drifted toward him.

When it made contact with his fingertips he felt a tiny, near-electrical tingling. When he blanked his mind and drew upon it for impressions, the sensation spread and he realized quickly that he was indeed reaching the other. Larick might be accused of carelessness, he mused, save that he had no way of knowing that Pol could still function in any magical capacity.

He followed Larick's progress through several turnings and up a long flight of stairs. There was a wide window at one turning, and he saw stars beyond it. Larick made his way through progressively more sumptuous areas of the keep, coming at last to a long gallery leading to a pair of ornate double doors. A liveried servant sat upon a bench to the right of the entrance. He rose as Larick approached, his face bearing a smile of recognition.

"Is he awake?" Larick inquired.

The man shook his head.

"I doubt it," he replied. "It's been a while—and he said he did not want to be disturbed."

"Oh. Well, if he should wake up, Mak, tell him that I've brought him the man he wanted."

"If he does, I will. But I don't think he'll be about again to-night."

"Then I'm going to see about getting the fellow fed now. Do you want anything sent up?"

"A bit of beef and bread would be nice, and maybe some beer."

"Ryle's turned in a little early . . ."

"The trip back tired him. He came rather fast."

"Don't tell me about it. All right. I'm for the kitchen. Good night."

" 'Night."

Pol followed him away from the place, step slower now, and down a back stair. He overheard him order the meals from a tired-looking fat woman of more than middle age, whom he had interrupted at a meal of her own, and then watched him prepare a light, cold dinner for himself and eat it quickly. Pol maintained the contact, his own hunger growing. On the fringes of things, he could see the woman preparing the trays.

Larick lingered over a second glass of wine, then sighed and rose slowly to his feet. He bade the woman good night, visited the latrine and made his way on, and downward, for a long distance into what must have been the northeastern wing of the place.

Pol continued his efforts to commit the route to memory, thinking that it must lead to Larick's own quarters. But it dropped lower and lower and seemed to lead farther and farther back toward the mountainside. All traces of splendor were gone here, and the area through which he passed bore the dustiness of disuse and seemed in places to have become a repository of damaged furniture.

Beyond this was a zone of dark emptiness where Larick created a light upon the tip of his blade and bore it overhead like a torch, coming at length to a bare and sweating rock wall over which he ran his hand. He followed this for a time, then turned into an opening in the rock, descending a steep slope into which rough steps had been hacked.

The way narrowed, grew level, turned. Larick began to slow. Twice again, it turned, and by then his steps were faltering. He was approaching a high, massy prominence with something possibly large and somewhat reflective atop it.

His hand wavered and the blade was lowered as he began to climb. Pol became aware that his breathing had deepened. Just as he reached the top he dropped to his knees and remained still. Pol

could not make out what it was that lay before him, for something
had suddenly gone wrong with the man's eyes.

He waited for a time, but nothing more happened, and then his
food arrived and he released the contact.

When he finished eating, Pol pushed the tray away and sought
the golden strand again. But it had either drifted off or dissipated.
He realized then that he should have affixed it to something, pend-
ing his later attention. Yet, he was tired, and he knew that he
would not be disturbed again till morning. He assembled a bed of
the sacking on the bench and stretched out, covering himself with
the blanket. He dozed almost immediately, myriads of images
from the past several days flashing behind his eyes.

These faded quickly, and that other consciousness came over
him again. There was a moment of intense cold, and then he stood
before the great Gate. He felt other presences at his back, but he
was unable to turn and look at them—nor did he desire to do so.
The right half of the Gate swung outward a sufficient distance for
him to angle through, tiny wisps of smoke or fog emerging from it.
This vision had occurred with a sharpness and a rapidity which
surpassed all earlier versions, and this time there was no ambiva-
lence, no hesitation on his part. He moved forward immediately
and entered the land which lay beyond.

The first thing that he saw, facing him, a short distance across
the blasted landscape, was the head. Impaled upon a sharpened
pole, eyes still open, the head of one of the demon creatures
leered in his direction. He felt that there was almost something
personal in this display, a very specific caution which he could
only at this time find amusing.

As he felt the transformation come over him, he winked at the
grisly visage and rose, wraith-like into the wan air. Wind-stirred
sands shifted snake-like among the rocks below him. He drifted
southward, gaining momentum rapidly. As he did, a sense of jubi-
lation grew within him until he wanted to proclaim it in a voice like
a thousand trumpets across the land. He spread his dark wings,
vast as the sails of some mighty vessel, and beat his way over the
deadland, rising to such an altitude that his mountains finally became visible.

He, Prodromolu, was filled with the dream-memory of his other
life, and he forgot the head and the Gate and the small human
thing named Pol Detson, of whom he might once have dreamed.
He needed none of these.

When he reached that range, he hurled himself upon it, fighting the hurricane-force winds that would dash him against it. Six times he assailed those heights and was beaten back.

On the seventh he prevailed, and his statue—dripping of honey and spices, of wine and of blood—was shattered at the Note that he uttered. Wherever his shadow passed, buildings toppled and his worshippers faded and died. Nyalith rose like a tower of dark fires before him. They met over the waters of the stilled ocean and commenced the dance that would take them around the world. Stars fell like burning souls about them, as the roaring winds bore them along the jewelled girdle of the planet. Their movements grew more savage with the deaths of kings and the fall of temples. He spoke again at the Mountains of Ice, and the Spell of the Gateway was wrought as Talkne, Serpent of the Still Waters, completed her journey of ten thousand years and rose from the depths to seek him—

Pol, for a moment, knew of the Keys and the dark god's promise as he was jerked suddenly alert there in his cell. The dream still vivid within him, he sat bolt upright and regarded the ghostly image of the woman who stood beside him, gesturing, lips moving, colorless eyes focussed upon his own. He half-rose, putting forth his hand.

She retreated, a look of sudden alarm upon her pale countenance. He withdrew, composing his face and making reassuring gestures. She halted. She appeared to study him. Slowly, she raised her arm and pointed at him. Then she turned and pointed toward the rear of the cell, turned back toward him and shook her head in the negative. He furrowed his brow and she repeated the motions. Suddenly then, she raised all five digits of her left hand and two upon her right. She shook her head, then went through the first series again. He shrugged and turned his palms upward.

She began to wring her hands. He rose, and she backed away. He took a step toward her, and she continued to retreat. He watched as she reached the far wall and passed through it, leaving behind perhaps the faintest trace of an exotic perfume.

He returned to his bench and seated himself, the entire sequence merging with his interrupted dream into a kind of hallucinatory half-world. Perhaps he had imagined it, he considered. Only her high cheekbones, large eyes, small chin and narrow span of brow beneath wide-swept wings of hair made such a strong, such a definite image. He sought, but she had left no strands behind by which he might test her reality.

He crossed to the door of the cell. For how long he had slept, he was not certain. He was still tired, but felt a little more rested than he had earlier. It seemed likely now that most others in the place would be asleep. Therefore, the time seemed good to depart, to commence investigating. He shifted to the second seeing to study the area about the door.

The response was slow, murky. It was as if he were wearing smoked glasses on a foggy day. He concentrated on the bar outside, on locating a connecting strand by which he might draw it.

Slowly, very slowly, a greenish strand came into focus—and passed out of it again. He called upon his dragonmark for power and willed that it return.

But the dragonmark did not throb. There was only a tingling, an itching sensation upon his forearm. The strand swam back into view and he reached for it. There was no contact. It passed through his fingers as if they were not present. Then it faded again. His eyes began to ache.

He lowered his hands. What was happening? he wondered. This was the first time in all of his experience in this land that the power had failed him. Could Larick have done something to block its flow?

Then he remembered what Larick had said about the initiation rite—that it might have this effect, that one should refrain from even the simplest workings for several weeks. Yet it had worked earlier, when he had followed Larick about Avinconet. It must be erratic during this period, he decided with a sigh. Somehow, he could hardly think of the injunction as applying to himself. His initiation had been a sham, a trap. Or had it? He had gone through all the motions, had undergone consciousness-heightening experiences at the proper times. Could it be that he had actually passed his initiation while being transformed into a monster?

He shook his head and tried again. His eyes ached more and his temples began to throb. There was a burning sensation along his right forearm. Once more, he saw the strand dimly, but he was unable to influence it.

He returned to the bench and covered himself. He thought of the woman for a long while before he slept again. And this time the only dream-image that he could later recall was the demon head on the stick, grinning.

IX.

In some ways I suppose that it was illuminating, though I am not actually certain how. It did something for me or to me, but I do not know what. It also served to make my nature more obscure to me in certain areas. Yet—

I had entered Belken, that great, dark, glittering, stone hulk, moving along the high tunnel I had found within. In the topmost chamber I brooded for a time, in the place of the waters. I felt a kind of power there, reverberating all about me. It was, in some ways, very disturbing; yet I found it soothing at other levels. I decided then to investigate the entire psychic structure within the mountain.

The route that the would-be sorcerers would take from station to station was clearly marked in non-physical terms. I proceeded to the second area and meditated for a long while in that place, also. If it did good things for them, charged as it was with a kind of ordering power, I reasoned that it might benefit me, too.

How long I took at that and the next station, I do not know. A long while, I believe, for I was lost in long reveries and quickly forgot all about time as I regarded their progressions. It only occurred to me that it might be growing late when I felt an increase in the levels of intensity of those forces in which I was basking. I quickly traced it back to its origin in a circle of sorcerers in the glittering city below. At that time I also learned that it had grown dark outside. I knew this meant that the initiation was about to begin and that the power would continue to rise all night long. I moved on to the next station to maintain my lead. I wanted to complete the thing now, for I felt it possible that it might shake something loose in my memory, giving me what I sought.

Something strange happened at that fourth station, for I heard a voice—tantalizingly familiar—speaking as if addressing me personally, intimately even.

"Faney," it said. "Faney."

It was a masculine voice, and it seemed to me as if I should understand exactly what it meant by that pronouncement. It was spoken fairly sternly, as if some order were being laid upon me. Faney. Was this my name, summoned from my faded past by the charged ambiance? No, that did not seem quite right. Faney . . .

"Faney!"—even stronger tones this time, and with them a roused sense of duty, a desire to follow the incomprehensible order and a sense of frustration at not being able to.

I expanded and contracted. I darted fitfully about within the chamber, seeking some means of discharging the injunction.

"Faney!"

Nothing. There was nothing that I could discover to do which would satisfy what was rapidly becoming a compulsion without an object.

So I moved on. And the power kept growing within the mountain. But the pressure was eased a bit in the next place, and I remained there for a long while. Again, I lost track of time and was only roused from a trance-like state into which I had lapsed by the sounds of the approaching candidates. Almost sluggishly, I drifted down to the next station so as not to be disturbed by them.

The sixth seemed more peaceful than any so far. I spread myself out and absorbed the good vibrations.

It did not seem that long before I heard them approaching again. This time I did not stir. I had no desire to depart and it occurred to me that it could be instructive to witness what went on in the course of the rites.

I watched them enter and take their positions. When he began speaking, I found myself peculiarly attracted to the one called Larick. I studied him, and then I realized why. It was an extraordinary discovery and I was still considering its effects when my attention was drawn to Pol. I was startled by the change in his appearance.

He was slouched well forward and his hands were enormous and scaly. A quick investigation beyond his garments showed me that his arms, though very attractive in their massive, dark fashion, were no longer *his* arms. Still, he could not be unaware of this, and if it did not bother him I did not see why it should bother me.

But it did.

Further examination showed me that he was the only one of all those present whose anatomy had been altered. As I puzzled over this, another transformation began in the area of his shoulders and breast. This time I was able to trace it to its source, and I saw that

Larick was causing it. I was unable to discover its motive in his mind, for a sorcerer's thoughts become impenetrable when he is working with the stuff of his trade. And none of the others' minds contained anything worth knowing; they were uniformly rapt in a kind of trance state.

I waited until they were finished there and moved on with them to the next station. Whether or not the motive would become clear to me, I was determined to investigate the method of the magical operation being practiced upon Pol.

I observed the next transformation very carefully and saw that it might more truly be considered a transference. As Pol's leg was replaced by a larger, more powerful version, I was able to trace the shifting of materials beyond the mountain. I followed, speeding and spinning down avenues where space was wrinkled and time a stream with many bends and some few oxbow lakes. I followed to the place of the Gate—that dream of Pol's which I had glimpsed. And I followed beyond, into the deadlands where I found a wailing creature whose body was now half-human, dragonmark upon the arm.

"Brother," I addressed it, "wear them well this short while, for it is but some human rite."

But it either could not or would not understand me. It continued its outcry and began beating at the transformed portions of its own person. So I laid a deep sleep upon it, there in the lee of a triangle of standing gray stones, serving both Pol and itself with little real effort on my own part. I told myself at the time that this was a necessary personal involvement—my first—in the affairs of others, for purposes of assuring that things be played out smoothly in their entirety, so as to satisfy a number of purely intellectual needs of my own.

But even then I was beginning to wonder.

I regarded that fascinating land for several extra instants before I swirled and began the long journey back, bright thunder and loud lightning oxymoronic over oxbows as I passed, passed I negative to reverse point and back, finding thoughts this time in Larick's head, of Avinconet and those he served. The first glimmer of understanding came to me.

I rotated with a certain satisfaction, then followed them to the next station. There, I saw the transference repeated with Pol's other leg. This annoyed me more than a little. His mind was as far asea as any of the others', convincing me that he was being victimized. It did not seem a very fair thing, judging from the little I knew about humans, especially coming from Larick the way that it was.

When we moved on to the next one, several things occurred in addition to the alteration of Pol's abdomen. The one candidate dropped dead. He, of course, was nothing to me; but at approximately the same moment there came a repetition of the word "Faney". I studied the others for reactions to this, but there were none. Of course, they had just acquired a dead man which might have proved distracting; still, it had sounded very loud, and after a few moments I heard it again.

And then again.

It became steady, relentless in repetition. At first I cowered, but then I listened. How silly of me to have thought that the others could hear it when it was so obviously addressing me and me alone. I felt that at some level I was beginning to understand it. And then something else occurred.

The body was moved, the ritual proceeded, Pol was altered. But none of these seemed particularly important at just that moment. I was undergoing a change, far less physical in nature than Pol's, a thing which raised fascinating and involved speculations on the subjects of free will and determinism. Unfortunately, I did not have time to pursue them just then, for my full attention was required by the change itself: I had changed my mind. I had taken an unstated, barely realized position of not interfering in the affairs of others for as long as I could remember. I suddenly brought it into focus, examined it and decided that the time had arrived to make an exception.

I did not like what was being done to Pol, but I did not possess the expertise necessary to reverse the phenomenon. I would do something, though—what, I was not certain—something to help him return to what was normal for him, so that he could deal with his own enemies as he saw fit.

I thought about it as we descended to the final station. The voice repeating "Faney" had faded. Pol predictably lost his feet at the next stop. I studied Larick in those moments when he was not conducting operations. I saw that he intended to spirit Pol off to Avinconet, where he would be a prisoner, as soon as the night's work was concluded.

When we departed the last station and moved on into the big cavern, I watched as he laid the paralysis upon Pol and began conducting the others outside. It seemed that I might be able to lift the spell which held him there in the alcove, but I was uncertain as to what could be done next.

I followed the first initiate outside, to witness the last phase of things. Then I saw that a number of the masters had come up to accompany their people back into town. Lurking in a secluded spot, Mouseglove watched the cavemouth.

Of course.

I was already working on my plan as I returned to the cavern. When I discovered the sorcerer of the midnight visitation with Pol, however, I halted and observed. There was a great feeling of power about the man.

He began using that power. I saw that he was employing it to reverse the transference. I moved immediately to interfere in a fashion which could not be detected. It was pure impulse on my part, not to see such good materials wasted. The creature's head could be mounted upon a stick by its fellows for all I cared. I made use of the drawstring space pocket as I had seen Pol do for storage purposes.

I saw Pol returned to himself and disguised. It in no way affected my plan when I realized what he intended to do. He would still be operating in an area of considerable danger.

So I sought the body of Krendel, the red-haired man who had died earlier. In that no one else was using it at the moment, I permeated it and set about studying how it worked. I wanted to have it ready soon to run the errand I had conceived of, to Mouseglove, who waited without.

X.

The small man slipped through the golden hole in the center of the room and it began to close behind him. A contracting halo, an optical aberration, the view through the opening was not that of the far side of the sumptuous apartment. Instead, the eye followed the dwindling form of the dark-clad man who had passed that way across a high tapestry-hung hall as it approached an arched gallery past pillars dark and light.

Then the wavering lens closed upon itself, flickered and was gone. Ibal slumped back upon the heap of cushions on which he had been sitting bolt upright. His breathing was suddenly deep and rapid; perspiration dotted his brow.

Vonnie, kneeling beside him, delicately blotted his face with a blue silk kerchief.

"There are not many," she said, "can do the door spell well."

He smiled.

"It is a strain," he acknowledged, "and, to tell the truth, not something I'd ever intended to work again. This time, though . . ."

". . . it was different," she finished.

He nodded.

"What are you going to do now?"

"Recover," he answered.

"You know that is not what I mean."

"All right. Recover and forget. I've given him a hand. My honor is satisfied."

"Is it? Really?"

He sighed.

"At my age, that is all the honor I can afford. The days are long gone when I would care to get involved in something like this."

Her hands passed through his hair, dropped to his well-muscled shoulders, rubbed there for a time, then led him back to a seated position. She raised a cool drink to his lips.

"How certain are you of your assessment of the case?" she finally inquired.

"The gods know what else it could be!" he said. "Something not at all natural sends Mouseglove to me, with the story that the young man I'd sponsored is old Det's son and that he's just been kidnaped by Ryle Merson. Honor says that I should do something because Ryle has made off with the man I sponsored. So I have. Fortunately, all Mouseglove wanted was a fast trip back to Rondoval—and I've just provided it."

"Is that really enough?"

"It is not as if he were my apprentice. I was only doing the man a favor. I barely know him."

"But—" she began.

"That is all," he replied.

"But it was not what I meant."

"What, then?"

"The things you said at first—could they be true?"

"I forget what I said."

"You said that it is a continuation of something that began before Pol was born . . ."

"I suppose that it is."

". . . the thing that had led to the wars."

He took the goblet into his hands and drained it.

"Yes, I believe so," he said then.

"Something that could reopen that whole business?"

He shrugged.

"Or close it. Yes. I think that might be the case—or that Ryle believes it might be the case. Same thing."

He set the goblet aside, raised his hands and looked at them.

"Pol has apparently aroused the concern of something powerful and supernatural," he said, "and he also has the good offices of the friend we just sent on his way."

"I was not talking about Pol. I am thinking of the entire situation of which that is but a part. This place is full of important practitioners of the Art. It is the only occasion in four years when they will all be together like this. I would almost say that it seems more than coincidental. Don't you feel that we ought to bring this to their attention?"

Ibal began to laugh.

"Stop and think about it for a minute," he said later. "I think it would be the worst possible thing to do. There were attractive things about both sides in that conflict. Some stood to benefit,

some did not. Do you really think we'd get a consensus? We can start the next war right here, if you'd like."

She had stiffened as he spoke and her eyes widened slightly.

"Gods!" she said. "You may be right!"

"So why don't we forget about the entire thing?" he finished. He reached out and took her hand. "And I know exactly how to go about it."

"I believe I'm getting a headache," she said.

Mouseglove did not look back. He accepted the sorcery which had brought him to Rondoval as a part of life. If magic were used against him, things could be very bad. If it worked to his benefit, he was grateful. Until he had met Pol, he had generally attempted to avoid the notice of sorcerers, counting them—usually correctly—as an untrustworthy lot. He mouthed a few words of thanks to Dwastir, patron of thieves, that this one had been helpful, as he hurried into the great hall and made his way down the stairway.

He located the bundle of faggots Pol had charmed for him, raised one and spoke the necessary words over it. He turned then and headed without hesitation along the confusion of tunnels, moving back toward the caverns where he had obtained more than one's normally allotted span of rest.

For a long while he passed through the cool places of dancing shadows before he reached the entranceway where the great slab Pol had toppled lay in shattered ruin all about.

Picking his way among the rubble, he continued into a place where the echoes died in the distance and the walls and roof were no longer visible, a place where the odor of the beasts hung heavy and the torch flickered in vagrant drafts. Here, too, he knew his way, and he proceeded along it with much less trepidation than he would have experienced some months earlier.

The vast, still mounds of scaled and furred bodies were sprawled casually about, many of them sleeping in the depths of magical charges as they had, he had, before. Some few others slept out their natural daily, weekly or monthly spans.

He wondered, as he made his way to the familiar niche, whether the one he sought would indeed be resting there. He might be any-where in the world, his absence necessitating Mouseglove's rous-ing another—a thought he did not relish. Having been trapped for twenty years in the same version of the sleep spell as Moonbird, he had developed a peculiar link—a thing even verging on friend-liness—with the giant dragon. With any of the others, he would have to attempt a complicated explanation, possibly beginning with his own identity. No, he did not like that thought at all.

As he came near to the place where Moonbird normally rested he grazed his shoulder against an unremembered rocky prominence.

Mouseglove! It has been long!

He stumbled back. It was a shoulder of dragon rather than a shoulder of stone against which he had brushed. He recovered almost immediately and moved to lay his hands upon the beast.

"Yes, I am back," he replied. "There is trouble. We need your help."

The great bulk shifted beneath his hands, causing them to slide along the hard, smooth scales. Moonbird began to rise.

What is it? he asked.

"We must go to Anvil Mountain, find Pol's scepter, take it to him."

He cast it into the fiery hole. He told me this.

"He told me, also—"

But I have been back, and the fires have died. All is gray rock now. I do not know how far I could dig in it. Get tools.

Mouseglove thought for a moment.

"There is a room off the main courtyard," he said, sending along the image. "I will return and look over the tools there. Meet me in the yard."

It will be faster for me to take you there.

"Well . . ."

Mount!

Mouseglove scrambled onto his back. Minutes later, they were gliding through the darkness.

XI.

Pol was awakened by the light shining upon his face. He tossed his head several times to avoid it, then sat suddenly upright, eyes opened.

The door of his cell stood wide.

Had someone come for him, then met with some momentary distraction? He listened. There were no sounds from the corridor.

Cautiously, he rose to his feet. He crossed the cell to the place where he had stood earlier, conjuring ineffectively, eyes throbbing. Some illusion? To torment him?

He extended his hand beyond the doorframe, touched the door. It moved slightly. At that moment, he felt the essence of mocking laughter, soundless. It was as if something vaguely sinister were amused at his puzzlement, his trepidation—something inhabiting a level of reality which did not coincide with his own. He stood frozen, waiting, but it did not occur again.

Finally, he moved forward, passing out into the corridor. It was deserted.

What now? he thought. Should he set out upon the route along which he had followed Larick? Should he strike out and explore elsewhere within the castle? Or should he head back to the courtyard, take one of the flying beasts and flee?

The latter course struck him as the most sensible: Flee, hide and wait for the return of his powers. Then he could go back to Rondoval, rouse his bestial minions and come back here as he had come to Anvil Mountain—to tear the place apart. It made better sense than remaining, powerless and outnumbered, in the citadel of an enemy.

He turned in the direction of the courtyard with the cages. Then he stood still.

His way was barred by a sheet of pale flame.

"And so my choice is not really a choice," he said softly.

Is it ever? came the familiar, ironic notes in his head.

"I guess that remains to be seen."

Like most things, came the reply, accompanied by slightly conciliatory sensations.

"I've never been able to figure out whether you're an enemy or an ally."

We are agents. We aided you once.

"And the next time . . . ?"

Why should you have any reason to doubt those who have helped you in the past?

"Because I came away with the feeling that I'd been pushed into something."

I would say, rather, that we pulled you out.

"That is a debatable point. But you say that you are agents. Agents of what?"

Change.

"Much is encompassed by that word. Could you be more specific?"

Two of the forces at work upon this world are science and magic. At times they are opposed to one another. We are on the side of the magic.

"This place hardly seems a stronghold of technology."

It is not. There is no direct confrontation involved here.

"God damn you! Getting a straight answer out of you is like milking a wildcat! Why can't you just tell me what is involved?"

The truth is such a sacred thing that we guard it well.

"I believe that you want my cooperation."

That is why we are assisting you again.

Pol tried shifting to the second seeing. This time it seemed to work smoothly. With it, he detected the outline of a human form within the flame—small, masculine, head bowed, hands hidden within the long sleeves which overlapped near its dark center. An orange strand drifted near Pol's right hand, the far end of it vanishing within the flame. He caught it with his fingertips and twirled it. The dragonmark throbbed upon his forearm.

"Now you will tell me what I wish to know—" he began.

His hand felt as if it were on fire. He stifled a scream and dropped to one knee in his agony. His second vision departed. His entire arm ached.

We will not be coerced in such a fashion, came the reply.

"I'll find the right way," he said through clenched teeth.

It would be so much easier and would save so much time if you would let us show you rather than spend the night telling you what is involved.

Pol rose to his feet, holding his aching right hand in the other. "I suppose that's the best deal I'll get from you tonight."

It is. Turn and follow the other.

Pol turned and beheld another tongue of flame. This one was only the size of his hand, and it hung in the air in the middle of the corridor about eight paces before him. A moment after his gaze fell upon it, it began to drift away from him. He followed.

It led him through a hall filled with grotesque statues, both human and non-human, a low, red brilliance, a soft, almost vibrant glow lying upon the whole setting, cast perhaps by the flame itself, giving the impression that all of the stone forms were beginning to stir. The air there was stale in his lungs, and he found himself holding his breath until he had departed the place. The luster was present in some of the other chambers and hallways, yet somehow it lacked the sinister character it had given to that room and those representations. The dragonmark had begun throbbing when they had entered the place and did not grow still until they were well away.

He moved down a series of stone stairways, each rougher than the preceding one, passing through damp chambers and long passageways, which, judging from the descent he had made, must be well beneath the castle itself and hacked from the living stone of the mountainside. At some point, Pol ventured a look behind him and saw that the other flame was nowhere in sight. He also saw, however, that the shadows seemed to slide in a liquid, almost sentient fashion at his back, in a manner he found more than a little unsettling. He hurried to keep pace with his guide.

The rooms and corridors through which he passed bore the dust of disuse in heavy layers, a thing he found mildly heartening when he moved through a series which could only be torture chambers—equipped as they were with chains, racks, tongs, pincers, weights, flails, whips, mallets and a great variety of oddly shaped blades. All of these bore stains, rust marks or both, along with the comforting coatings of dust. There were bones in odd corners, all of them gnawed long ago by rodents, now dry, brittle, cracked and discolored. Pol brushed a wall with his fingertips and heard the echoes of screams from long ago. When he switched to the second vision, he caught near-subliminal glimpses of atrocities enacted in times gone by, the traumas of which had etched themselves into the setting. Hastily, he reverted to the normal mode of seeing.

"Who . . ." he whispered, more to himself, "was responsible for these things?"

The present lord, Ryle Merson, came the reply from ahead.

"He must be a monster!"

Once, such things were routine here. But he ceased all such activities nearly a quarter of a century ago, claiming that he had repented. It is said that he has led a relatively blameless, possibly even virtuous life since.

"Is it true?"

Who can say what lies in a person's heart? Perhaps he cannot even say himself, for certain.

"You are making this all totally enigmatic to me. I confess to being prejudiced, but in no way can I see his treatment of me as virtuous or blameless—and that goes for his lackey, Larick, as well."

People have reasons for things that they do. Motives and objectives are seldom of matching moral color.

"And what of yourself, whatever you are?"

We are neither moral nor immoral now, for our actions contain no element of choice.

"Yet something set you upon the course you follow. There was a decision there."

*So it would seem—*a touch of irony to these words?

"Still not giving anything away, are you?"

Nothing.

They moved past a fetid-smelling cistern in which something was splashing. The floor of a recess near an adjacent airshaft was heavy with the droppings and fragile, hieroglyphic skeletons of what might have been bats. Indentations in the floor contained small pools of water. The walls were slimy in this area, and Pol felt as if a great weight of earth and rock hovered just above his head, groaning the long, slow notes of timeless stresses.

He wondered at the brief conversation, recalling the allegations of the Seven after the battle at Anvil Mountain, giving the impression then that their actions were determined. At least they were consistent in what little they did say. There was something more about them which he felt that he should remember, something almost dream-like in texture . . .

His efforts at recollection ended as he turned a corner and halted. Whether it was a corridor or a room which he now faced, he could not tell. The way ahead was misty—almost smoky—though he detected no odors about it. The flame had halted when he did, and it seemed much nearer now; its brightness had increased, and it had acquired something of a greenish cast.

"What the hell," Pol asked, "is that?"

Just a local etheric disturbance.

"I don't believe in ether."

Then call it something else. Perhaps you will be footnoted by some future lexicographer. We know that things were different where you grew up.

"I'll be damned. That's the closest I've come to getting a rise out of you. So you know my history?"

We were present when you departed this world. We were present when you returned.

"Interesting. Your remarks almost lead me to believe that you do not know what things were like in the place where I was raised."

True, though we are able to conclude a number of things about it from examining your actions and reactions since your return. For example, the familiarity with technology which you demonstrated—

The light before him was extinguished. Pol stood still in the semi-darkness, staring into the faintly luminous mist. He listened to his heartbeat and considered calling upon the dragonlight.

An instant later a blue leaf of flame appeared in the air before him, near to the place where the other had been.

Come now!

The tone was feminine, imperious.

"What became of my other guide?" he asked.

He talked too much. Come!

Pol wondered at this. Had he finally glimpsed a chink in their armor?

"Getting near something you don't want me to know, eh?"

There was no reply. The blue flame began drifting slowly away from him. Pol did not move to follow it.

"Do you know what I think?" he said. "I think that you've got to use me because I am my father's son and he created you. You have some special connection with Rondoval, and only I can serve your purpose."

The flame halted and hovered.

You are wrong.

"I do not believe that you like this," he went on, ignoring the response, "because, for all your talk of determinism, I was raised on another world about which you know little or nothing, and you cannot account for me as you might someone who'd spent his life in this land. I am more of a random factor than you would like me to be, but you have to deal with me anyway. Tonight you will attempt to impress me in some fashion so that I will be more amenable to your purposes. I tell you now that I have seen things beside which the display at Anvil Mountain was very small beer. I am prepared to be unimpressed by any efforts on your part."

You have finished?

"For now."

Then let us continue this journey.

The flame drifted on, slowly. Pol followed. It seemed to be bearing to the left, but there were no other objects in his field of vision against which he might track its motion. He plodded along, and the palely illuminated mist rolled and boiled about him. Unaccountable shadows began to move within it.

He kept changing direction. Echoes were muffled. Pol could not tell for certain whether he was moving through a long, twisting corridor or whether he was backtracking, turning, wandering within one large room. As he was unable to locate any walls, he suspected the latter. But there seemed no way to tell for certain.

The shadows which tracked him grew darker, their outlines becoming more distinct. Some were definitely human in form; others were not. The silhouette of a dragon flickered overhead as if passing at a great height. It seemed as if a great number of people were now moving, silently, at various distances, about him. He tried turning to the second seeing, but there was no change in the prospect.

Suddenly, a figure loomed directly before him—big, ruddy, balding, with large, capable hands. The flame darted past, and perhaps it took up a station somewhere nearby.

"Dad!" Pol said, halting.

His step-father's mouth twisted into a half-grin.

"What the hell do you think you're doing in this backward place?" he said. "I really need you at home, in the business, right now."

"You're not real . . ." Pol said.

But Michael Chain looked solid. His facial expressions—his speech inflections—were exactly those of Michael Chain with a few drinks under his belt and a load of impatience about to break loose.

"You're a disappointment to me. Always were."

"Dad . . . ?"

"Go on with your silly games then. Break your mother's heart."

A gesture of dismissal. The large man turned away.

"Dad! Wait!"

He vanished into the mist.

"It's a trick!" Pol said, glaring at the flame. "I don't know how you did that or what it's all about, but it's a trick!"

Life is full of tricks. Life itself may be a trick.

He turned away.

"Why are we standing here in the gloom? I thought you were taking me someplace important?"

You are the one who halted.

"Okay! Let's get going!"

He turned back.

Betty Lewis, wearing a tight, low-cut dress, stood frowning at him off to the left. The texture of her familiar flesh looked so real . . .

"You could have called," she said. "Maybe it wasn't that big a thing between us, but you might at least have said good-bye."

"I couldn't," he answered. "There was no way."

"Just like all the others," she said, and the mists moved between them and she was gone.

"I see what you are doing," Pol said to the flame. "But it won't work."

It is the condition of this place. You are doing it to yourself.

Pol took a step forward.

"You brought me here!"

"Pol?" came a familiar voice from his right, sending a shiver along his arms.

"The hell with you!" he said, not turning. "Let's go, flame!"

Obediently, the bluish light moved away, and he followed it. The shadow remained to his right, drew nearer.

"Pol!"

He did not look. But an arm was extended into his field of vision—muscular, covered with heavy, rust-colored hair, a thick, wide bracelet at the wrist, studded with control buttons, indicators, lights—and even when he saw it, he did not believe that it was real.

Until the hand fell upon his arm, gripping it, halting him, turning him.

"I feel your hand," he said slowly.

"I felt your wrath," said the other.

Pol raised his eyes to regard the once handsome, rugged features of Mark Marakson, marred by the eyepiece to the left, its lens a deep, glittering blue.

"You gave me no choice," Pol replied.

"You had my name, my parents. You took my girl . . ."

"This can't be!" Pol said.

". . . my life," Mark finished, and then the lens went black and his flesh reddened and charred and began to peel away.

Pol screamed.

The hand, through which the bones were now visible, fell away from his arm. The figure backed off into the mist—the black-lensed prosthetic now affixed to a skull—and then it was gone.

Pol began to shake. He raised his hands to his face and lowered them again.

Nora now stood where Mark had been. Her face was expressionless.

"It is true," she said. "You killed the man I loved."

She turned and walked away.

"Wait!"

He ran, reaching for her, but her shadow was lost among others. Still he groped, turned, moving in one direction and then another.

"Come back!"

Pol! Stand still! Do not lose yourself in this place!

He turned again, and old Mor stood before him, leaning upon his staff.

"For that which I see before you, I would that I had never brought you back," the sorcerer said. "Better Mark had prevailed than that you do the thing you would do."

"I don't know what you're talking about," Pol said. "Tell me, if there is something I should know!"

Mor vanished in a burst of fire.

Stay with me! came the words out of the flame. *This could get out of control!*

"Whose control?" Pol asked, turning away.

Stel, the centaur, stood looking into his eyes.

"You would break faith with us," she said, "though you swore by your scepter not to."

"I have not broken faith with you," he replied.

". . . And the doom which walks always at your back will move forward."

"I have not broken faith," he repeated.

"Evil son of an evil father!"

Pol turned and strode away.

Come back!—almost, a pleading note now.

The giant dog-headed figure he had faced beneath the pyramid rose suddenly before him.

Thief! Breaker of the Triangle of Int! came its mental message.

"I stole nothing. I took what was mine," Pol said.

I've curses for thieves, to hound them to the ends of the earth!

"Piss on your curses!" Pol replied. "I beat you once. I'm not afraid of you now!"

He took a step toward the menacing figure.

Stop! They're gaining power! It really can hurt you! came the words out of the flame which had just appeared between them, sounding frantic now.

The dog-headed one raised his right arm. Pol wheeled and ran.

Stop!

A small shape rushed into view. It was white, had long ears, was wearing a waistcoat. Its nose twitched.

"Late again!" it said. "It'll be my head, sure as hell!"

It looked up at Pol.

"Yours, too," it said, before it scurried off.

Pol kept moving.

Stand still! In this place—

He almost bumped into the man. It was the nameless sorcerer he had fought back at Rondoval. Pol backed away from him.

The sorcerer raised his right hand and a fiery knife appeared within it. He cast it directly at Pol's breast.

Pol threw himself to the side and hit the ground rolling. He continued the movement until he was well away from the place.

He lay panting for several moments, then moved to regain his feet. Another man approached as he did so, moving quickly, halting before him. It was a tall, regal figure, with a single black streak running back through a mane of white hair. Pol realized immediately that the features were very similar to his own.

"You are . . . ?" Pol said.

"Det Morson, your father," came the reply.

"Well curse me and be on your way," Pol said, standing. "That's the game here, isn't it?"

"I am not a part of the game here. I am merely taking advantage of it." His right hand rose and brushed Pol's cheek lightly. "Whichever way you turn, no matter what your decision, no matter how things break," he said, "your real enemy will be the Mad-wand."

"What Madwand? I thought that was a general term for—"

"Henry Spier is the greatest of the Madwands, and he is known only as that."

"What kind of name is Henry Spier? In this place—"

The tongue of flame flared into being between them.

Back, Det! Back to your special hells! came the voice out of fire. *Your power over us has passed!*

Det raised his hands, crossing his arms upon his breast. As if by contagion, flames violated his outline. Suddenly, however, he raised his head and stared at Pol.

"Belphanior," he said. "Remember that in time of need."

Pol opened his mouth to question him, but Det was gone in a rush of fire and wind.

The flame which hung before him began to contract, resuming its former, smaller size and shape.

What did he mean by that? it asked him.

"I have no idea," Pol answered.

What else did he tell you?

"Nothing. There wasn't time."

You are lying.

"The truth is such a sacred thing that I guard it well."

The flame did not move. He felt sensations of puzzlement and of anger, but no words came with them. Long moments passed.

Finally, with a movement almost like a shrug, the flame drifted leftward. Pol followed. There were still shadows in the mist, but they did not draw near. The flame moved quickly now, and Pol increased his pace.

The mist began to thin. Pol saw a wall to his left, nothing to his right. Shortly; an archway appeared before him. He followed the light through it and felt as if he had returned to normal space. There was no mist on this side, only dimness and a faint odor of mildewed tapestry.

"We were really just moving around inside one big room, weren't we?" Pol asked.

There was no reply.

"It was a kind of downbeat Rorschach-thing, wasn't it?" he said. "Everything in there came from me, one way or another. Didn't it?"

Silence again.

"Okay," he said, as they approached a stairway leading upward. "If whatever you want from me requires my cooperation, just remember that you haven't been keeping the customer happy."

He reached the stair and began to mount it.

A ripple of amusement passed back down over him. His drag-onmark throbbed intermittently. They reached the top of the stair and passed through a better-furnished, though apparently long-unused room. After exiting, they came upon another stair, again leading upward. As he climbed it, Pol reflected that they had probably come into that eastern or northeastern wing of the place into which he had followed Larick's progress earlier.

"We've taken a kind of roundabout course, haven't we?" he said.

It was necessary.

"Why?"

To avoid the inhabited sections.

"Is that the only reason?"

Why else?

"Not to condition me or impress me in any fashion?"

You flatter yourself.

"Have it your way."

We will.

He took a lefthand turning and headed along a narrow corridor. Then a right into a room with a single, large window which faced out across the ramparts onto a bleak, starlit landscape. The room itself contained old and damaged furniture not arranged as if for use. He exited at its farther end and entered another room also obviously being used for storage. Pol brushed away the strands of a spiderweb as he passed. A rat dashed across his path and crouched, staring, beneath an armchair.

Two rooms later, in a place with several doors, a feeling of familiarity came over him. He felt certain that Larick had passed this way earlier.

His feelings of fatigue were rising again as they headed leftward and back from corridor to tunnel to a place where rough-cut steps led downward. The flame moved faster, grew brighter now. He increased his pace to match it, reaching out as he passed to touch the rock wall, discovering it to be as moist as it appeared. Yes, this was the way that Larick had come.

He hurried about the turnings and there, finally, before him, was the dark, stony rise with the shining thing atop it. The flame rose toward it. Pol climbed after.

"What is it?" he said under his breath.

Something we'll need.

"You're so damned helpful."

Far more than you seem to realize.

A little later, he saw that it was a casket with a bulging, transparent cover. And when he came up beside it, he drew in his breath sharply, for he saw that it held the body of a woman, perfectly preserved. Her high cheekbones, small chin and wings of hair he now saw to be of a light brown color in the glow shed by his guide, were not unfamiliar to him.

"The ghost . . ." he breathed.

Her spirit is said to wander these halls. It is of no importance. Remove the lid.

"How?"

There are fasteners along the sides and at either end.

Pol continued to regard the pale features.

"Why the Snow White bit?" he finally asked.

Pardon? I do not understand the reference.

"Why is she on display?"

Her father, Ryle Merson, wishes to view her upon occasion.

"Morbid son of a bitch, isn't he? I suppose he's laid a preserving spell on her—if she's been dead very long."

It has been a long while. Remove the lid.

"Why?"

In order to move her.

"Why move her?"

Her presence is required elsewhere. Do as we say!

"All right. It was a pretty steep climb, though."

You will bring her this way.

The flame brightened and Pol could see a level ledge beyond the casket, leading back toward a tunnel. He leaned forward and sought the fastenings. One by one, he undid them and slipped them. He seized hold of the lid's frame then and strained to raise it. For a time, it resisted his efforts. Then, with a creaking sound, it slid slowly upward.

He eased the transparent cover back and lowered it to the ground. Only then did he pause to scrutinize the woman with more than clinical concern.

"What's her name?" he asked.

Taisa. Pick her up. Bring her this way.

The flame advanced along the level route beyond the casket.

Pol stooped, raised the woman in his arms. The faint, familiar aroma of a delicate perfume reached his nostrils.

"How did she come to this end?" Pol asked, as he moved around the catafalque and followed.

A victim of circumstance, in a long and involved struggle.

He crossed the ledge and entered the tunnel behind the moving light.

It turned abruptly to the left after a few paces, and Pol found himself traveling upslope. The feeling of anticipation which had been his companion since he had awakened, was heightened now. He felt that he was nearing the heart of a mystery, a mystery made very personal, a mystery in which he would be playing a significant role.

Another turn, and he was in a wide, high, partly furnished room carved out of stone. A large rectangular opening in the lefthand wall showed stars in a now pale sky, and the upper slopes of the mountain. There were heavy chairs and a long table toward the front of the place. To the rear . . .

He halted and stared.

Bring her over here.

Slowly, almost mechanically, his limbs moved to obey. He was barely aware of the motion, his eyes locked upon the revelation set into the far wall.

Set her down there. No. The head at the other end.

Pol placed Taisa's body atop a slanting stone slab, her feet at the higher end. Her head fell into place within a wide channel which had been cut into the hard, gray surface. Automatically, he adjusted her long, simple, blue garment about her. As he did, he noticed a wide, shallow basin below the end of the groove. A dagger of black stone lay upon its rim. These things registered but made no real impression upon him, for his attention was focussed elsewhere.

He stared at the wall before him, at the great double doors set within it. Perspiration dampened his brow, and his hands possessed a slight tremor as he moved away from the woman and the stone, staring.

They were the Gate of all the forgotten dreams which fell like bright cloaks upon him now.

He drew nearer. The doors were solid, massive, ironbound, and of a dark, metallic-looking wood. There seemed to be no locking mechanism, no handles, only the intermittently spaced rings.

Carved and burned into the Gate in an elaborate coiled pattern, rising from the base to the midpoint, was the form of an enormous serpent, drawing itself high above a stylized line of waves. Three heavy spikes had been driven into it—one at the neck, one at the tail and one at the body's middle.

Then, raising his gaze to the top of the frame and above it, he beheld the familiar form of a great, black bird-like thing, wings outspread, carved into the rock. And into this figure, also, spikes had been driven—one into either wing.

Pol took another step and halted, breathing heavily. He was again Prodromolu, Opener of the Way, coursing the heavens of Qod, while below him, mounting steadily upward from the depths, the serpent Talkne moved upon the final circuit of her eons-long journey in search of him. Nyalith shrieked a warning which shattered mountains and revealed the secrets at their hearts. Wheeling, he dove toward calm sea-surface . . .

He came to himself once more, remembering the Keys and the dark god's promise to lead the people from the devastated land, to merge that place with another by opening the way between the worlds. And the Keys . . .

The Keys!

The statuettes were the Keys. Strangely living Keys . . . And—

He lowered his eyes.

Yes . . .

Incised into the floor and painted in fading yellow, red and blue was a large, irregularly shaped diagram. A section of it swept back to encompass the slab upon which Taisa lay; another portion projected far forward, touching the Gates' heavy frame at the left. A number of sharp, near-triangular segments were extended, thorn-like, from the main body of the design. Suddenly aware that his dragonmark was throbbing slowly and heavily, Pol counted them.

". . . Five, six, seven."

Exactly.

He barely glanced at the flame, which hovered now above Taisa.

Bring our physical representations into being upon this plane now, and place each of us at one of the points. You know the order.

"Yes."

Pol shifted his vision, raised his right hand, caught one of the seven ebon strands leading back over his right shoulder. He rotated his hand, winding the filament about it until he felt a tension upon it. The power flashed from his dragonmark back along the line and he jerked upon it.

He held one of the statuettes in his hand—tall, slim, feminine, sharp-featured and imperious. Its cloak bore a patina of beaten gold and it was girdled with orange, red and yellow stones. A single green gem was set into its forehead.

It felt warm and grew warmer yet as Pol held it, turning his head.

Yes . . .

He moved to his right, setting it at the tip of the second peak from the end, facing toward the Gate.

As he straightened, he saw that the stars were fading, the sky growing brighter.

He raised his hand, seeking the strands again. They were not apparent. He realized then that his vision had slipped out of the second seeing. He strove to shift it back, but to no avail.

His dragonmark, he noted then, had lost its recent throbs of power. He massaged his forearm. He tried again to recall his vision.

What is the matter?

"I don't know. I can't do it."

What do you mean you can't do it? You just did.

"I know. But something's slipped again. The power has been coming and going since I went through Belken. Right now it's gone."

The flame moved toward him, hovered directly before his eyes. He closed them against the brightness.

Keep your eyes open.

He obeyed, squinting. He saw that the flame was growing, was becoming a vast sheet of fire, now his own size, now larger.

It advanced and he drew back.

Stand still. We must investigate.

It wrapped him like a cloak, it settled upon him. He felt that it was penetrating his body, his very being. There was no sensation of heat, only an odd, vibrating feeling, as when one steps ashore after several days at sea.

Abruptly, it was gone and a shrinking flame swayed before him.

It is true. You are not at the moment capable of functioning at a magical level. There is no way of telling how long this will last, and the night is almost ended. Ryle Merson may send for you in

*the morning. We must abandon the project for now and secure
you once more within your cell. Return the statuette and—*

Pol shook his head slowly.

*Of course. In your condition, you cannot return it; and we are
barred from exercising any direct control over our analogues. Pick
it up. We passed a number of rocks and niches on the way in here.
You will have to hide it.*

"What about Taisa?"

Leave her.

"What if someone finds her here?"

Not important. Come.

The flame moved past him. He picked up the statuette and followed it. Back in the tunnel, he found a place to cache it in a cleft
in the rocky wall.

They made their way out of the cave and back into the palace
proper. After a few turnings, Pol realized that they were moving
along a different route than they had taken earlier. Their progress
was much more rapid this time, avoiding the misty chamber and
the dark tunnels entirely.

In a short while, he found himself back at his cell and he entered there, drawing the door closed behind him.

"The journey over was just for show, wasn't it?" he said.

Go back to sleep now.

The flame winked out. He heard the bar slide into place. Suddenly overwhelmed with fatigue, his head spinning, he staggered
to his bench and collapsed upon it. There was no time to think
before the dark waves took him . . .

XII.

Henry Spier disguised himself anew as he departed the caves of Belken and returned to the enchanted city at its foot. There he spent the day in celebration among his fellow sorcerers, none of whom knew his true identity. He delighted in walking among them bearing a great, dark secret none of them shared. He drank wine spiced with delicate narcotics and he worked wonders and avoided only the greatest among his colleagues. There were none that he feared in a conflict of wills, but he did not wish to come under the scrutiny of any master great enough to pierce his disguise. No, that would be a premature revelation.

He walked, scattering curses and dooms upon those of whom he disapproved, tossing in an occasional boon for one who had won his respect. It pleased him no end to play this secret, god-like role. He had refrained for so long. But now—Now he saw the future loosening upon its branch above his outstretched hand. He felt a strange, overwhelming kinship for those who were about to benefit from his labors, all unknowing.

The city expanded in magnificence as the day waned. He had not felt this fine in years. His powers reached an incredible pitch, but he restrained himself from demonstrating more than a fraction of their potency to new comrades gathered round for games and trials.

He hummed and danced as the night descended. He labored over an enormous and elaborate dinner until well past midnight. He brushed sleep away and renewed his vigor with a spell of high order, realized simply and quickly. He drifted upon a silver barge on the town's circular canal, taking with him a courtesan, a catamite, a succubus, a bowl of smouldering dream-leaf and a jug of his favorite wine, which renewed itself as rapidly as its master. After all these years of obscurity and disguise, there was call for celebration, for the Balance was about to tip.

The night wore on, and the city became a fantasia of light and color, sound and senses-dazzling magic. He continued his revels until the sky paled in the east and a momentary hush fled like a phantom wave across the shapes-shifting jewel of the city, to break at the foot of Belken. The night's activities commenced again immediately thereafter, but a certain spirit had gone out of them.

Shaking the dust of dream and passion from his person, he rose from his scented cushions and put aside the lighter pastimes of the night. Shedding all frivolity and growing in size as well as regality of mien as he walked, he departed the livelier precincts of the city, heading northward. When he reached the fringe of the city's charmed circle he passed on, climbing a low hill. At its summit, he paused, head lowered, turning.

Finally, he stooped and picked up a dry stick with a number of small twigs still attached. He caressed it and began speaking softly, introducing it to the four corners of the world. Then he stared at it in silence for a long while, still stroking it slowly. The morning grew brighter as he did this, and when he knelt to place the stick upon the ground, it appeared that it had altered its shape, coming now to resemble the form of a small animal. He commenced a low chant.

"Eohippus, Mesohippus, Protohippus, Hipparion . . ." it began.

Dust and sand rose from the ground to swirl about the small figure in a counterclockwise direction, obscuring it completely. As he continued, the spinning tower rose and widened into a dark vortex far larger than himself. It produced a low moaning sound which rapidly became a roaring. Materials from greater and greater distances were sucked into it—shrubs, gravel, bones, lichen.

He stepped back away from its tugging force, arms raised to shoulder level, hands rising and falling. A long, wavering cry came from its center, and he moved his hands downward.

The roaring ceased with a blurt. The swirling curtain began to fall away, revealing a large, dark, quadrapedal outline, head high and tossing.

He moved forward and placed his hand upon the neck of the creature, unfamiliar to the inhabitants of this world. It whinnied.

A moment later, it grew calm, and his hand slid back to the pommel of the saddle with which it had come equipped. He mounted and took up the reins.

They were at the center of a crater which had not been present when he had begun his spell. He spoke to the sand-colored beast, rubbing its neck and its ears. Then he shook the reins gently.

© JUDY KING RIENIETS 81

It climbed slowly out of the depression and he turned its head northward. He smiled as they began moving in that direction. Scarlet fingers reached above them from out of the east as they made their way down to a more level area and located a trail. He squeezed with his knees and rustled the reins again.

"Hi-yo, Dust!" he shouted. "Away!"

His tireless mount shot forward across the dawn, quickly achieving a blinding, unnatural pace.

XIII.

They had arrived in the afternoon, Mouseglove and Moonbird, circling above the wreckage atop Anvil Mountain. Looking downward, Mouseglove, who had spent so much time there, found it difficult to recognize those features he had known. But he saw the one huge crater, still now, beside the wreckage of a tall building.

"That has to be it," he stated, "the place where Pol said he cast the rod."

It is, Moonbird replied.

"It is said that the eye of a dragon sees more than the eye of a man."

It is said correctly.

"Any of the machines or the dwarfs still active down there?"

I see no movements of either sort.

"Then let us go down."

To the crater?

"Yes. Land beside the cone. I'll climb it and have a look."

It is quiet within it. And I do not see excessive heat.

"You can see heat?"

I ride on towers of heat when I soar. Yes. I am able to see it.

"Then take us down inside, if you know it is safe."

Moonbird began a downward spiral toward the flared opening. He tightened his turnings as they drew nearer, then drew in his wings and dropped, spreading them at the last moment to ease the landing slightly. Gritting his teeth, Mouseglove had watched the rough gray walls rush by. He was jolted forward and to the side when they struck the irregular surface. Clutching at Moonbird, he turned a fall into a dismounting movement, then stood upon the slagheap, leaning against the dragon's swelling ribcage. There was a great silence, and shadows already cloaked the declivity.

Moonbird turned his head from side to side, then looked up, then down.

I might have made a small miscalculation, the dragon confessed.

"What do you mean?"

The size of this place. I may not have sufficient room to climb into the air.

"Oh. Then what are we to do?"

Climb out when the time comes.

Mouseglove cursed softly.

There is a brighter side to the matter.

"Tell me."

The scepter is definitely here. The massive head turned. *Over that way.*

"How do you know?"

Dragons can also sense the presence of magic, of magical items. I know that it is below the ground. Over there.

Mouseglove turned and stared.

"Show me."

Moonbird moved with a slithering sound across the gray roughness, the rubble. Finally, he halted, extended his left forelimb and with an enormous black claw scored an X upon the dark surface.

You must dig here.

Mouseglove unloaded the digging implements, selected the pickaxe and attacked the spot indicated. Chips flew in all directions, and he coughed occasionally from the dust he raised. He removed his cloak and finally his shirt, as the perspiration flowed freely. After a time, he assumed a statue-like aspect as a layer of gray dust clung to his body. His shoulders began to ache and his hands grew sore, as he drove the pit to a shin-deep level.

"Does your dragon-sense," he asked then, "tell you how deeply it is buried?"

It lies somewhere between two and three times your height in depth.

The crater returned ringing echoes as Mouseglove threw down the pickaxe.

"Why didn't you tell me that sooner?"

I did not realize it was important. A pause. Then, *Is it?*

"Yes! There is no way I can dig down that far in any reasonable period of time."

He seated himself on a mass of rubble and wiped his brow with the heel of his hand. His mouth tasted of ashes. Everything smelled of ashes. Moonbird moved nearer and stared into the shallow pit.

Might there not still be strong tools about? Or weapons? From the time when Red Mark ruled here?

Mouseglove raised his eyes slowly until he was staring directly overhead.

"I suppose I could climb out and go looking," he said. "But supposing I found some explosives—or one of those throwers of light beams which cut through things? It might destroy what I am seeking."

Moonbird snorted and his spittle flew about. Wherever it struck it began to boil and smoulder. After several seconds, each moist spot burst into flame.

The thing was once hidden because no one knew how to destroy it.

"That is true . . . And I'm certainly not making much progress this way."

He picked up his cloak and began wiping the dust from himself on its inner surface. When he had finished, he donned his shirt again.

"All right. I think I remember where some of the things were stored. If they are still there. If I can still find my way—in all this mess."

He moved to what appeared to be the most negotiable face of the crater wall. Moonbird followed him, with rough sliding sounds.

I had better begin climbing out myself.

"It looks pretty steep, for one of your bulk."

You go now. I will come up in my time. I wish to be away from the disturbance.

"Good idea. I'm on my way."

Mouseglove found a handhold, a foothold, commenced his climb. Later, when he paused to rest upon the rim and looked back down, he saw that Moonbird had made scant progress in his attempt to scale the wall. He groped slowly and carefully for the perfect hold, then dug in with his powerful talons, improving each niche or shelf with deep gouges before trusting his weight to it.

Mouseglove turned away, surveying the area once again. Yes, he decided. Over there to the southeast. . . . One of the places where I hid was beneath that leaning monolith. And . . .

He glanced at the sinking sun to take the measure of remaining daylight. Then he moved with speed and grace, descending, circling, every step of his route already in mind.

He moved among twisted girders and blocks of stone, craters and smashed war machines, heaps of rubble, shards of glass, the skeletons of dragons and men. The ruined city was very dry.

Nothing grew. Nothing moved but shadows. He remembered his days as a fugitive in this place, still reflexively casting an eye skyward for sign of the birdlike mechanical flyers, still sliding about corners and automatically checking for spy devices. For him, the giant figure of Mark Marakson still stalked the broken landscape, his one eye clicking and flashing through all the colors of the rainbow as he moved from darkness to light to shadow and back again into darkness.

Crossing the fire-scored pavement beside one of the fallen bridges, he ducked through a twisted doorframe into a roofless building. Within, he passed the shriveled bodies of half a dozen of Mark's diminutive subjects. (He resented the term "dwarf" by which the others referred to them, since he was approximately the same height himself.) He wondered as he went by what it might be like for any survivors of that engagement—to be raised from barbarism to a highly organized level of existence and then to be cast back down again to subsisting as in days gone by, all the machines stopped. Perhaps it had been too brief an interlude, he told himself. They would not yet have lost their primitive skills. This entire experience might merely turn to the stuff of legend among them one day.

But from somewhere—he was never to be certain where—he seemed to hear the sound of hammering; and twice, he heard the chuffing noises which made him think of attempts to start one of the great machines.

He located the stairwell he had been seeking and spent ten minutes clearing it for his descent. Below, he followed a series of twisting tunnels down into the mountain itself, the turnings as fresh in his memory as if he had traversed them but yesterday, despite the fact that he moved now through regions of absolute blackness—the generators which had provided their minimal lighting having long since failed. He moved with a certain deliberation, his pistol in his hand. But nothing threatened him here.

The door to the arsenal was locked, but he was able to pick it in the dark, his sensitive fingers faultlessly manipulating the small pieces of metal he had always with him. They had a memory of their own, his fingers, and he had opened this lock before.

Inside, then. And he crossed the room and sought the racks. He filled a grenade belt and slung it, pausing only to acquire an extra supply of cartridges for his pistol after this was done.

Departing the place, he halted and for reasons not completely clear to himself, locked the door. Then he hurried back along the tunnels, gripping the pistol once again.

As he mounted the stair, a touch of panic—immediately suppressed—followed by a full measure of heightened alertness, came to him. What subliminal cues might have triggered this response, he did not know, but he trusted it fully because it had served him well in the past. He halted, pressed against the wall, then commenced moving slowly up the stairway, his footsteps grown soundless through deliberate placement.

When his head cleared floor level, he halted again and studied the interior of the wrecked room. Nothing stirred. The place seemed unchanged since his earlier passage.

He drew a deep breath, mounted the remaining steps quickly and headed toward the doorway.

There was a rapid movement to his right.

He halted when he saw that it was one of the short, heavily muscled aboriginals who had manned this place, emerged from behind a slanting piece of cracked ceiling material, moving so as to bar his way. The man had on the tattered remains of the uniform those in Mark's service had worn.

Mouseglove raised the pistol and hesitated.

The dwarf was armed with a long, curved blade. But it was not the inequality of arms which stayed Mouseglove's trigger finger. The man appeared to be unaccompanied, but if there were others about the sounds of gunfire might summon them.

"No problem," Mouseglove ventured, lowering his weapon and thrusting it away. "I'm just leaving."

Even before the other's wide mouth shaped a grin, he'd a feeling that he would not be able to talk his way out of this one.

"You were one of them," the man said, moving toward him, blade twitching. "Friend of the sorcerer . . ."

Mouseglove dropped into a crouch, his right hand falling upon the hilt of the dagger which protruded from his boot-sheath, his thumb unfastening the small strap which held it in place.

Still bent far forward, he took the weapon into his hand and began a sidewise, shuffling movement toward his right. The other advanced and slashed at his head with the curving blade. Mouseglove avoided it and raised his own weapon quickly, to nick the man's forearm. He sidled faster and feinted twice toward the man's chest, dodged a thrust he knew he would be unable to parry and produced a small laceration in the other's brow above the right eye with the crosspiece of his own blade. It should have been

© JUDY KING RIENIETS 81

a neat slash, but he had underestimated the man's speed. The sudden contact with the horny brow-ridge threw him slightly off-balance and he retreated, stumbling.

He recovered his balance, but continued the stumbling movement to scoop up a handful of broken masonry.

Straightening, he cast the pieces at the other's head, danced to the right and thrust. He attempted to twist the blade as it entered the man's left side but found that he was unable to withdraw it.

The man pushed him away and swung his own blade. Mouseglove darted out of range, snatched up another piece of masonry, hurled it and missed. The man moved toward him, the dagger protruding from his side, his blade still raised, his face expressionless. Mouseglove could not tell how much strength remained with him. Another rush, perhaps . . . ? It would be too risky to turn his back on him now, or attempt to dart by—and he still effectively barred his way to the door. He considered simply attempting to avoid him until the injury took its toll. The man had not raised an outcry, and Mouseglove was still determined not to use the pistol unless all else failed or an alarm was given.

The other seemed to smile, tight-lipped, as he came toward him, and Mouseglove realized that he was being backed toward an outhouse-sized slab of roofing material.

"I will live," the dwarf said. "I will recover from this. But you—"

He rushed, blade raised high, careless of any openings now.

Mouseglove gripped the heavy grenade belt which hung from his shoulders, dropped low and swung it with all of his strength toward the other's legs.

The man toppled and Mouseglove moved. He did not spring, because the other had managed to raise his blade. But he seized the extended wrist and threw his weight upon it, covering the fallen man with his own body, pushing downward. With his other hand he caught hold of the other half of the blade and twisted, so that the cutting edge was turned.

As he leaned, pushing it toward the other's throat, the man's left hand clawed upward toward his face. He ducked his head and drew back; as he did this, he felt the other's legs locking about him. They tightened almost immediately, achieving a painful pressure. As this occurred, the left hand assailed his face again, fingers raking toward his eyes.

He removed his right hand from the blade and raised it to fend off the attacking hand. As he did so, the right hand began to move upward against his pressure, the blade slowly turning. The other's

legs continued to tighten until he felt that his pelvis would surely
crack. Now, slowly, teeth clenched, the man began to raise his
wide shoulders from the ground.

Mouseglove dropped his defending right arm and drove the
elbow down and back against the haft of his blade which protruded from the other's side.

The man shuddered and fell back, the grip of his legs loosening.
Mouseglove repeated the blow and a moan escaped the man's lips.

Then Mouseglove's right hand was upon the other's blade
again, as he dragged himself free and threw his weight forward.
The blade sank rapidly, its cutting edge touching the other's wind-
pipe and continuing downward.

As the blood spurted, he dragged the weapon across the throat
and still held tightly to it, afraid to let go until long after a series
of spasms had shaken the man, to be followed by a stillness, despite the fact that his hands, arms and shirtfront were spattered
and in places soaked by the other's blood.

He wrenched the blade away then and cast it aside. He rose
and, placing his foot upon the body, drew his dagger from it and
wiped it upon the man's garments. He sheathed it, picked up the
grenade belt and slung it over his shoulder, drew his pistol again
and departed the wrecked building.

Nothing barred his way as he headed for the crater, and he
began feeling that his assailant had been a solitary survivor, half-
crazed perhaps, scratching out a living and leading a reclusive life
among the remains of the previous year's debacle. But then he
began hearing noises—a falling stone, a metallic creaking, a
scratching, a shuffling sound—any one of which might, by itself, be
taken as the action of settling, or wind, or rodents. Together, however, and coming upon the heels of his struggle, they acquired a
more sinister aspect.

Mouseglove hurried, and the sounds seemed to follow him. He
scrutinized every bit of cover as he went, but detected no one—
nothing—of a threatening nature. The sounds, however, increased
in frequency behind him.

He was running, however, by the time he reached the base of
the cone, and he commenced climbing immediately, not even
looking back. And though he scanned the rim of the crater, there
was no sign of Moonbird at the top.

As he climbed, he heard the footfalls below, behind him. A
backward glance took in six or eight of the small people, emerging
from the ruins, running after him now. While they bore clubs,

spears and blades, he was slightly relieved to see that none of
Mark's advanced weapons appeared to have survived for their use.
Several of them, he noted, wore bits of machined metal, like amu-
lets, about their necks. At that moment, he wondered how much
they had really understood of the technology into and out of
which they had been so quickly propelled. The speculation was
only a fleeting thing, however, accompanied as it was by the acknowledgement that primitive weapons render one just as dead as
the more sophisticated variety.

Climbing, he wondered then concerning the ghostly bond which
permitted him to communicate with Moonbird. Their proximity
and spell-involvement in the caves of Rondoval during the two
decades of the spell's effect had worked that linkage. He had never
communicated with the dragon except at close range, though it occurred to him that now only a thin layer of rock might be all that
separated them.

Moonbird! Do you hear me? he cried out in his mind.

Yes, came a distant-seeming reply.

Where are you?

Climbing. Still climbing.

I'm in trouble.

What kind of trouble?

I'm being pursued, Mouseglove told him, *by those people who
worked for Mark.*

How many?

Six. Eight. Maybe more.

How unfortunate.

There is nothing that you can do?

Not from here.

What shall I do?

Climb fast.

Mouseglove cursed and looked back. All of his pursuers were
nearing the cone's base—and one heavily muscled man was drawing back his spear for a cast. Mouseglove drew his pistol and fired
it at him. He missed, but apparently spoiled the other's aim. The
spear flew wide, clattering against the cone far off to his right.

He fired again, and this time the nearest of his pursuers
dropped his club and clutched at his right shoulder.

What was that?

I had to shoot at a couple, Mouseglove replied, remaining low,
continuing up the slope.

Did you find what you sought?

Yes. I have explosives. But my pursuers are too scattered to make them an effective weapon.

But you can use them from a distance?

Yes.

When you reach the top throw them down to the place you dug. How far up are you?

That is not important.

They make quite a blast.

It should be amusing. Not worry.

Mouseglove looked back again. Three of his pursuers had reached the base of the cone and were beginning to climb. Halting, he took careful aim and fired at the foremost. The man fell.

He did not pause to assess the effect of this upon the others, but turned and put his full strength into his ascent. He was nearing the top now. His pursuers were strong and agile, but so was he. He also weighed less and was faster, so he had managed to acquire a good lead.

Finally, he reached the rim and mounted it, passing over its lip immediately, for cover. Only then did he look down. He made a soft noise at the back of his throat.

Moonbird, dragging his ponderous bulk slowly up the steep wall, had only succeeded in climbing about a quarter of the distance to the top.

I can't throw these things, he told the dragon. *You're too near.*

I have flown through thunderstorms, came the reply, *when the heavens came apart all around. Yet I lived. Throw them.*

I can't.

We die if you do not. And Pol . . .

Mouseglove thought of his pursuers, primed one of the grenades and hurled it down toward the now darkened area where he had been digging earlier. He covered his ears. He heard the blast and felt the vibration. Afterward, he heard the sounds of falling and shifting rocks.

Moonbird! Are you all right?

Yes. Throw another. Hurry!

Mouseglove complied and braced himself again. After the second explosion, he inquired: *Moonbird?*

Yes. Another.

The reply seemed slightly weaker, or could it but have been the roaring in his head, submerging it? He threw the third explosive, pressing himself back against the stone until the detonation occurred and the force of the aftershock had abated.

Moonbird?

There was no answer. He peered downward, through the clouds of dust and the shadows. The area where Moonbird had clung was now totally obscured.

Answer me, Moonbird!

Nothing.

As the ringing in his ears subsided, he thought that he heard scraping noises of ascent from the outer surface of the cone, though they could possibly have been the sounds of falling rocks. He dared not cast a grenade back over the lip of the crater because of its possible effects upon himself, there on the inside.

Quickly, he began his descent.

The dust irritated his eyes and nose, though he was able to refrain from sneezing. He tasted it and he felt particles of grit when he clenched his teeth. He spat several times but could not rid himself of it completely. His way darkened perceptibly with every movement of descent.

His eyes turned regularly in the direction of the area Moonbird had occupied, but he could detect no sign of the great dragon in the darkness below.

Mouseglove continued his descent, wishing, as he groped after a new foothold, that there were some manner in which he could manage to move more rapidly. For now the foremost of the small men was lowering himself over the edge above and two others were moving to follow. Just as he was about to look away, he saw a fourth figure come up and join them.

Cursing, he reached for the next lower hold. Before his hand located it, however, the rest of his body detected a faint, general vibration in the rock to which he clung. A rumbling sound followed.

Below him, waxing and waning but brightening in the overall process, an orange glow had begun in the heart of the crater. The growling noise came again, accompanied by a wave of heat.

There was a shout above him. His pursuers—five now—had halted. They began climbing upward as he watched, their movements touched with panic.

My bombs tore something loose, he decided. It's starting again. Can't go up. Can't go down. Wait and die.

Come down. You will not be harmed.

It's going to erupt!

No. Come down. You will be safe.

What—What is happening?

Can't talk. You come.

Mouseglove's hand continued its long-interrupted motion, coming to rest upon a stony knob to which he transferred his weight.

As he descended, the light grew brighter. The vibrations continued, but they were extremely mild, almost an effect of the echoes which bounced about him. Suddenly, with a roar, a bright fragment of something shot upward past him, followed almost immediately by another, tracing glowing trails through the twilight high above.

Are you sure it is safe? he asked, pressed tightly against the rock wall.

But there was no reply.

Continuing downward, he realized that the temperature had not risen excessively, as might be expected this near the point of an eruption. Could Moonbird be playing games with his own flames, to frighten off the enemy?

No, he decided, looking down into the glow. It covers too large an area and burns too regularly to be dragonfire.

He reached the floor of the crater unharmed. Clots of fire continued to flee upward, but none rose from points near him. Walls and pillars of flame came up in great number here, though what it was they fed upon, he could not discern. There was a clear aisle through their midst, however, heading in the direction he intended to take. He followed it.

The floor of the crater was even more ravaged than he remembered it, as a result of his bombing. He picked his way through heavy rubble toward the heart of a large depression as he headed for the site of his earlier digging. After several more steps, he realized that a vast shadow loomed at its center, below him.

He took another step.

Moonbird . . . ?

It swayed in his direction, and he saw the great head of the dragon nodding toward him, an ornate rod held between the enormous teeth.

The scepter! You've found it!

Mouseglove extended his hand.

Get onto my back.

I do not understand.

Talk later. Mount!

Mouseglove advanced and climbed upon Moonbird, scrambling toward his shoulders. Immediately, the dragon began to move, climbing out of the pit, heading toward the northern wall, almost exactly opposite the place he had climbed earlier.

When they reached the crater wall, Mouseglove suddenly caught hold more tightly as Moonbird reared and commenced climbing.

Moonbird! You can't get to the top from here! It gets almost vertical about halfway up.

I know.

Then why are we climbing?

It is easier here. Till then.

But—

Wait till we reach the ledge.

Mouseglove recalled the rocky shelf to which he referred. It had looked wide enough to support Moonbird—barely—but it was, in effect, a deadend.

Moonbird was climbing much more rapidly here than he had up the other wall. The way was less steep, more rugged. As they mounted higher, Mouseglove glanced back down. The glow from the fires below seemed to be spreading, intensifying. He felt a wave of heat upon his face. It was followed almost immediately by another, much warmer.

At last, Moonbird reached the rocky shelf, hauled himself onto it, turned and looked downward. As he did so, the brightness and the heat increased again.

"What is happening?" Mouseglove asked aloud.

The last explosion shook me from the wall, Moonbird replied. *After I fell I sensed the rod nearby.*

"And the fires started about that time?"

I started the fires. To drive off your pursuers.

"How did you do that?"

I used the bottom segment of the rod. It is for fire magic.

"You can use the rod? I had no idea—"

Only the bottom segment. Dragons understand the secrets of fire.

"Well, we seem to be safe now, but the fires keep getting stronger. You might turn them off now—if you can."

No.

"Why not?"

I will need a tower of heat. To rise out of here.

"I do not understand."

I will dive from here toward the fires. It is easier to ride the warm air upward.

Shadows were dancing all about them now. Mouseglove felt a fresh wave of heat.

© JUDY KING RIENIETS 81

"It's not all that far to the bottom . . ." he said. "Are you sure you can get yourself airborne in that distance?"

Life is uncertain, Moonbird replied. *Hold tightly.*

He spread his wings and plunged into the blazing crater.

XIV.

The depth of my philosophical speculations as to the nature of my own being and that of the universe only increases the more I see of the world. And no real answers seem to occur, either practically or on a more general level. I now find myself wondering whether a state of uncertainty might not be the lot of all sentient beings. Still, it strikes me that there are reasons I do not fully comprehend underlying the actions of others. Their activities seem directed toward creating certain situations, whereas I have no real —objectives. I circulate. I obtain information. But I have no idea what it all means. I do not have an objective, only its mysterious ghost—something which keeps haunting me with the notion that I should have more.

Despite my perplexity in the face of existence, I continued to obey the small imperative which had accompanied me since my departure from Rondoval. I saw Mouseglove off on his errand and watched to see that Ibal did indeed possess the means to deliver him to his destination expeditiously—not to mention the will to do it. I observed Mouseglove's departure and then returned to the place at the foot of Belken where I had obtained my first lessons in animating a body. I tried it again with the spare, with good results, frightening a group of hikers made up of a number of the younger apprentices.

Then I hovered undecided. Should I follow the still-discernible emanation trail of that strange sorcerer back into the city, to discover what he was about? Or should I undertake the pursuit of Pol and Larick toward Avinconet in the north? Almost immediately, that small imperative resolved the matter.

I rose, achieving some altitude, resolved myself into a tighter form, then headed approximately northward. I overtook them in their flight and simply paced them then, drifting, for the rest of the day. Nothing was answered for me by this, but I no longer felt the pressures I had experienced earlier. For this time, I was as content as I had been in the old days, moving aimlessly about the ruins of Rondoval.

Of course it could not last. I realized this as the day wore on and the light was squeezed from it and the great castle, Avinconet, loomed before us in the darkening distance. In that moment, I learned the feeling of fear.

A strange foreboding came over me—a dark premonition, if you like—accompanied by the seeming sourceless knowledge that I could die, that my existence could be terminated and that this thing could occur within that place. It was something which had never occurred to me before, and it came as an awful revelation—for even as I considered it along with what I knew of myself, I saw that it could well be true. It would seem that a life as aimless as mine, more filled with questions than anything else, might not be worth much. I realized in that same moment that this was not the case. More than anything else, I felt, I wanted to continue it, as purposeless and puzzling as it seemed.

I drew nearer to Pol. I wrapped myself about the warmth of his being. Why the thought of flight did not even occur to me at that time, I had no idea. I clung to him as a child to a parent as we rushed nearer that dark citadel.

I remained with him after we landed, accompanying him to the cell in which he was confined. I remained there with him for some time—until his food arrived and I realized that it was unlikely he would be disturbed for the rest of the night. While my earlier fears had not been abated, they had receded sufficiently by this time to permit more rational considerations to come to the fore. Now, while all was still and nothing seemed afoot, would actually be the best time for me to survey the place, to locate whatever menaces might be lurking and consider the best means to nullify them.

Accordingly, I drifted away, leaving Pol in his safe and uninteresting quarters. I moved about various chambers, terminating rats and mice, observing sleepers, seeking signs of dark magics or dangerous forces.

I moved very slowly, not wishing to be surprised. The night wore on, and I came gradually to feel that I had suffered a false augury. Nothing threatened, nothing loomed. It seemed just another pile of rocks made suitable for human habitation by the application of a few simple construction principles and the installation of simple plumbing, some rude pieces of furniture and garish hangings of a nonfunctional nature. The only traces of magical doings seemed painfully innocuous.

Yet, feeling what I had felt, I was not to be so simply discouraged. The middle of the night drew on and passed. I explored each high tower. I—

An indescribable pang passed through my being. It was like nothing I had ever experienced before, unless it be the unremembered shock of my own birth. Something had suddenly changed, something affecting me to the depths of my personality. But even as it occurred, I grew doubtful that it was the fearful thing I'd sought. No tone of dark magic accompanied it. Its ultimate result was a sense of something having been settled in my own case. If I could but discover what it was, I felt that a part of my personal mystery might be solved. I drifted for a long while, meditating, but no illumination ensued and I could not determine the source of whatever it was that had come over me. It was almost as if, somewhere, my name had been spoken, just out of my hearing.

I settled, descending from floor to floor. I had investigated most of what lay above the ground and I decided to regard the areas below the castle, within the mountainside. There were a number of openings, both natural and artificial, and one by one I invaded them and explored.

It was in one of these recesses that I came upon the sleeping woman. She lay unmoving within a container, her spirit wandering, a very pale light of life still visible about her. I moved nearer, to inspect her further, and a trap was sprung. It was a subtle spell, designed to ensnare any less than material being such as myself who might venture too near the lady—presumably to protect her against possession.

So I was caught, several body-lengths from her, in what might best be described as a gigantic, invisible spiderweb. I struggled briefly and saw that it was to no avail. I relaxed against my bonds and tried altering my shape. This did not work either, nor did my attempts to shift away to another plane. The web of forces held me tightly.

I hung, spread out there, trying to analyze it. It had a certain aura of venerability about it, of the sort humans ascribe to vintage wines. I was familiar with this effect from my experience with certain old spells which remained about Rondoval. The good ones, such as this, unfortunately grow better with age, because of the counter-current entropy on the plane where magic operates. This spell, as nearly as I could judge, went back fifteen or twenty years. I tried sending charges of energy through it, a small segment at a time, hoping to locate a weakness at which I might work, from which I might unravel the thing like a stocking. All to no avail. It was of a piece, and it had me.

I remained there for a long while, recalling everything I knew that might be applied against it. When I tried them all and nothing worked, I decided that it might be time to cultivate philosophy to a greater extent. I began musing upon existence and non-existence, I reexamined my premonition, I reconsidered my pang . . .

I heard footsteps.

It is generally easy to remain inconspicuous when you are invisible and soundless, but I made extra efforts to achieve stillness on all levels, including the mental, when I saw Pol approaching led by a peculiar palm of light as immaterial as myself.

There was something familiar about the flame-like thing, something I did not like at all. I felt, without knowing why, that it had the power to harm me.

I sensed some exchange going on between Pol and the brightness. I heard only Pol's half of it, not willing to try attuning myself to listen in fully, fearing that this might somehow make my presence known to the fiery one.

Finally, Pol unfastened the lid of the container, removed it and set it aside. There was another long pause, and then he removed the woman, crossed a ledge and entered a tunnel, following the flame.

Suddenly, I was free. The spell must have been centered upon the woman, not the locale, not the container.

I hung back. I wanted to see where they were going but I did not wish to get too near, lest I be trapped again. I drifted slowly behind them, leaving myself ample leeway, well aware now of the effective range of the spell.

I recognized the big chamber as soon as I entered it. The last time I had passed this way, I had been moving at metaphysical speeds and following a magical trail, so there had been no need for noting landmarks. Consequently, I'd had no idea that this was where the Gate was located.

The Gate . . .

Just as I remembered it, from Pol's dreams and from my own fast passage, the Gate loomed huge, threatening and, fortunately, closed. It had never been opened upon this plane, I guessed, though its ghostly version had been ajar many times, permitting the passage of sendings, essences, spirits. Had its physical self stood so, it might not be possible to close it again, for I could see how an interpenetration of the worlds would begin, the strangely structured, more ancient forms of that other with its vastly stronger magics flowing through to dominate this younger, magically weaker land, changing it into something of its own image, re-vivified by the raw, natural forms of this newer place. Stronger in magic, weaker in general vitality. The magic would dominate, I was certain . . .

Pol deposited his burden upon the stone with the aura of death about it. His movements were slow, irresolute, as if he were walk-ing in his sleep. I reached out carefully then, more carefully than anything I had ever done before, and I touched his mind, just skimming his surface thoughts.

He was bewitched. He was not aware of it, but the flame had him in thrall.

I saw no way that I might interfere successfully. I knew without knowing how I knew that the thing was stronger than me. I felt to-tally helpless as it led Pol about, as it directed him to produce the statuette. I was more than a little pleased when Pol's power failed and the project had to be abandoned. The flame's frustration gave rise to the closest thing to joy that I had ever known.

I watched them depart. I doubted that Pol was in any immedi-ate danger, and I wanted to explore the chamber a little further. A large, rectangular piece of morning decorated the wall to my left. I began to feel a fresh premonition, concerning this room.

XV.

Pol was awakened from a dreamless sleep by the sound of his cell door being unbarred. At first he felt leaden-limbed, hung over, ragged about the edges of his mind, almost as if he had been drugged. But then, within moments, before Larick had even set foot in his cell, the dragonmark began to throb wildly, heavily, in a way it had never done before, sending an adrenalinlike shock through his entire system, clearing his head instantly, informing him with a sense of wild power unlike anything he had known previously.

"Get up," Larick said, approaching him.

Pol felt that he could strike the man dead with a single gesture. Instead, he complied.

"Come with me."

Pol followed him out of the cell, adopting the cumbersome, lumbering gait suitable, he'd judged, for a disguised monster. Through the first window they passed, Pol saw that full daylight now lay upon the world, though he could not see the sun to judge the hour. They took a different route than that upon which he had magically followed Larick the previous evening—different, too, than the way upon which the flame had led him.

"If you cooperate," Larick said almost casually, "it is possible that you will be released unharmed."

"I do not consider myself unharmed," Pol said, mounting a stair.

"Your present situation might be remedied."

"What's in this for you?" he asked.

The other was silent for a long while. Then, "You would not understand," Larick said.

"Try me."

"No. It's not for me to explain things to you," he finally answered. "You will have your explanations shortly."

"What is the price for betraying the trust of the initiation committee?"

"Some things are more important than others. You'll see."

Pol chuckled softly. The power continued to spiral within him. He was amazed that the other could not feel its presence. He had to restrain himself from lashing out with it.

They traversed a lengthy corridor, mounted another stair, crossed a wide hall.

"I would like to have met you under different circumstances," Larick said then, as they reached a downward stair.

"I've a feeling that you will," Pol replied.

He recognized an area through which he had passed during the night. He realized then that they had come into the northeastern wing of the building. They approached a dark, heavily carved door. Larick moved ahead and knocked upon it.

"Come in," came a voice slightly higher in pitch than Pol had expected.

Larick opened the door and stepped across the threshold. He turned.

"Come along."

Pol followed him into the room. It was a study in rough timbers and stone, with four red and black rugs upon the floor. There were no windows. Ryle Merson was seated at a large table, the remains of his breakfast before him. He did not rise.

"Here is that Madwand we discussed," Larick said. "He is completely docile in all but spirit."

"Then you've got the part that counts," Ryle replied. "Leave him to me."

"Yes."

"I mean it literally."

Pol saw the look of surprise which widened Larick's eyes and parted his lips.

"You want me to go?"

Ryle's broad face was expressionless.

"If you please."

Larick stiffened.

"Very well," he said.

He turned toward the door.

"But stay within hailing distance."

Larick looked back, nodded curtly and departed the room, closing the door behind him.

Ryle studied Pol.

"I saw you at Belken," he said at length.

"And I saw you," Pol said, returning the older man's stare.

"On the street, talking with Larick, in front of the cafe where I
sat."

"You have a good memory."

Pol shook his head.

"I can't recall giving you cause for abduction and abuse."

"I suppose it must look that way to you."

"I suppose it would look that way to anybody."

"I don't want to start off with you on the wrong foot—"

"I didn't want to start off with you on any foot. What do you
want?"

Ryle sighed.

"All right. If that is the way it must be. You are my prisoner.
You are in jeopardy. I am in a position to grant you any discomfort, up to and including death."

The fat sorcerer rose, moving around the table to stand before
Pol. He made a simple gesture and followed it with another, his
movements similar to those Larick had used. Pol felt nothing,
though he realized what was occurring and he wondered whether
the disguise within the disguise would hold.

It did.

"Perhaps you have grown fond of your present condition?"

"Not really."

"Your face is masked by your own spell. I will leave it in place,
since I already know what you look like. I suppose we could start
with that."

"You've a captive audience. Go ahead."

"Last year I heard a rumor that Rondoval was inhabited again.
A little later, I heard of the battle at Anvil Mountain. By magical
means, I summoned up your likeness. Your hair, your birthmark,
your resemblance to Det—it was obvious that you were a member
of that House, and one of whom I had never heard."

"And of course you had to do something about it, since nobody
likes Rondoval."

Ryle turned away, padded across the room, turned back.

"You tempt me to agree and let it go at that," he said. "But I
have reasons for the things that I do. Would you care to hear
them?"

"Of course."

"There was a time when Det was a very good friend of mine.
He was your father, wasn't he?"

"Yes."

"Where did he have you hidden, anyway?"

Pol shook his head.

"He didn't. As I understand the story, I was present at the fall of Rondoval. Rather than slay a baby, old Mor took me to another world, where I grew up."

"Yes, I can see that. Interesting. For whom did he exchange you?"

"Mark Marakson, the man I killed at Anvil Mountain."

"Fascinating. A changeling. How did you get back here?"

"Mor returned me. To deal with Mark. So you knew my father?"

"Yes. We engaged in a number of enterprises together. He was a very accomplished sorcerer."

"You speak as if there was a point where you ceased being friends."

"True. We finally disagreed on a very fundamental issue concerning our last great project. I broke the fellowship at that time and sent him packing. It was then that he initiated the actions which led to the conflict and the destruction of Rondoval. The third party to our enterprise left him when things began looking bad on that front."

"Who was that?"

"A strange Madwand of great power. I don't really know where Det found him. A man named Henry Spier. Odd name, that."

"Do you mean that if you both hadn't deserted him Rondoval might have stood?"

"I am sure that it would have, in a cruelly changed world. I prefer thinking that Det and Spier deserted me."

"Of course. And now you want some extra revenge on the family, for old times' sake."

"Hardly. But now it is your turn to answer a few. You say that Mor brought you back?"

" 'Returned me' is what I said. He did not accompany me. He seemed ill. I believe that he went back to the place where I had been."

"The exchange . . . Yes. Were you returned directly to Rondoval?"

"No. I found my own way there, later."

"And your heritage? All the things that you know of the Art? How did you come by this?"

"I just sort of picked it up."

"That makes you a Madwand."

"So I've heard. You still haven't told me what you want."

"Blood tells, though, doesn't it?" Ryle said sharply.

Pol studied the man's face. Gone now was the bland expression which had accompanied most of their earlier exchanges. Pol read menace in the narrow-eyed look now focussed upon him, in the rising color and the tightness about the mouth. He noted, too, that one pudgy hand was clenched so tightly that its rings cut deeply into the flesh.

"I don't know what you mean," Pol said.

"I think you do," Ryle replied. "Your father tipped the Balance which prevailed in this world, but did not succeed in his attempt. I stopped him here and Klaithe's forces finished him at Rondoval. There had to be a reaction sooner or later. Mark Marakson brought it into the world at Anvil Mountain, where you stopped him. Now it must tip in the other direction again—your father's way—toward total sorcerous domination of the world. It can be stopped for good at this point, or it can go all the way—your father's dream realized. I have been waiting all these years to stop it again, to end it, to see that it does not come to pass."

"I repeat. I don't know what—"

Ryle came forward and slapped him. Pol fought down an impulse to strike back as he felt a ring cut his cheek.

"Son of a black magician! You are one yourself!" he cried. "It can't be helped! It's in your blood! Even—" He grew silent. He stepped back. Then, "You would open the Gate," he said. "You would complete your father's great work for this world."

Pol suddenly felt that this was true. The Gate . . . Of course. He had forgotten. All those dreams . . . They began phasing now into his consciousness. With this, a certain wiliness came over him.

"You say that you were party to the entire business, at its beginning?" he asked softly.

"Yes, that is true," Ryle admitted.

"And you were talking about black magic . . ."

Ryle looked away, walked back to the table, drew the chair farther back and lowered himself onto it.

"Yes," he said, his eyes directed toward the remains of his breakfast, "in both senses, too, I suppose. Black because it was being used for something that was morally objectionable, and black in the more subtle sense of its deepest meaning—the use of forces which must warp the character of the magician himself. The first is always arguable, but the second is not. I admit that I was once a black magician, but I am no longer. I reformed myself long ago."

"Employing Larick to perform the actual spells for you hardly seems to avoid the spirit of black magic. As in my case . . ."

His words trailed off as Ryle raised his eyes and fixed him with them.

"In your case," he said, "I would—and will, if necessary—do it myself. It would at worst be an instance of the first sort—employed to prevent a greater evil."

"On the general theory of morals—that others need them?"

"I am thinking of more than the two of us. I am thinking of what you would do to the entire world."

"By opening the Gate?"

"Exactly."

"Excuse my ignorance, but what will happen if the Gate is opened?"

"This world would be flooded, submerged, by the forces of a far older world—in our terms it is an evil place. We would become an extension of that land. Its more powerful, ancient magic would completely overwhelm the natural laws which hold here. This would become a realm of dark enchantment."

"The evil may well be relative then. Tell me what objection a sorcerer could have to something which would make sorcery more important."

"You use the argument by which your father first swayed me. But then I learned that the forces released would be so strong that no ordinary sorcerer could control them. We would all be at the mercy of those others from beyond the Gate and those few of our own kind to whom it would not matter, in league with those others."

"And who might those few of our own kind be?"

"Your father was one, Henry Spier another; yourself, and those others like you—Madwands all."

Pol repressed a smile.

"I take it that you are not a Madwand?"

"No, I had to learn my skills the hard way."

"I begin to understand your conversion," Pol said, instantly regretting the words as he saw Ryle's expression change again.

"No, I do not believe that you do," he answered, glaring, "not having a daughter bound by the curse of Henry Spier."

"The ghost of this place . . . ?" Pol said.

"Her body lies in a hidden spot, neither dead nor alive. Spier did that when I broke the fellowship. Even so, I was willing to fight them."

Pol wanted to look away, to shift his weight, to pace, to depart. Instead, "What exactly do you mean when you say Madwand?" he asked.

"Those like yourself with a natural aptitude for the Art," Ryle said, "those possessed of a closer, more personal relationship with its forces—its artists rather than its technicians, I suppose."

"I appreciate your explaining all these matters," Pol told him, "and I realize you are not going to believe any denials I might make concerning my intentions, so I won't make any. Why not just tell me what it is that you want?"

"You have had dreams," Ryle said flatly.

"Well, yes . . ."

"Dreams," he continued, "which I sent to you, wherein your spirit traveled beyond the Gate to witness the starkness and desolation of that evil place, wherein you saw the creatures who dwell there, engaged in depravities."

Pol recalled his earlier dreams, but he thought too of the later ones, showing him the cities beyond the mountains, neither stark nor desolate, but holding a culture so complex as to surpass his understanding."

"That is all that you showed me?" he asked, puzzled.

"All? Is that not enough? Enough to persuade any decent man that the Gate must not be opened?"

"I suppose you made a good case then," Pol said. "But tell me, are dreams all that you sent to me?"

Ryle cocked his head to one side, frowning. Then he smiled.

"Oh. That," he said. "Keth . . ."

"Keth? He was the sorcerer who attacked me in my own library?"

Ryle nodded.

"The same. Yes, I sent him. A good man. I thought he'd best you and settle things then and there."

"What things? For all your talk about the Gate and my father and Madwands and black magic, I still do not know what it is that you want of me."

The fat sorcerer sighed.

"I thought that by sending you the dreams—showing you the menace of the thing—and then by explaining the situation carefully, as I have just done, that I might—just possibly might—win you

over to my way of thinking and persuade you to cooperate with
me. It would make life so much easier."

"You didn't exactly start off on the right foot by playing monster games with my anatomy."

"It was also necessary to show you the extent to which I will go
if you do not choose to help me."

"I'm still not sure of that. What's left—besides death?"

Ryle rubbed his hands together and smiled.

"Your head, of course," he said. "I have begun in the easiest
manner possible. But if, after suitable painful practices upon the
body you are now wearing, you refuse to give me what I want,
then I will complete the transfer. I will send your head to join the
rest of you in exile beyond the Gate. I will be left with a somewhat maimed demon servant, and you—you have seen that place—
you will have an unfortunate existence before you for all your
remaining days."

"It sounds very persuasive," Pol observed. "Now, of what
might it be the consequence?"

"You know where the Keys are—the Keys that can open the
Gate or lock it forever. I want them."

"Presumably to do the latter?"

"Certainly."

"I'm sorry, but I don't have any such Keys. I wouldn't even
know where to look for them."

"How can you say that when I saw them on the table in your
study numerous times—and even as I watched your struggle with
Keth?"

Pol's thoughts went back, both to that scene and to one of his
dreams. He felt the resistance building within him.

"You can't have them," he said.

"I'd a feeling this was not going to be easy," Ryle remarked,
rising. "If opening the Gate means that much to you, it just shows
how far gone you really are."

"It is not opening the Gate," Pol replied. "It is having something taken from me in this fashion that rankles. You are going to
have to work for anything you get out of me."

Ryle raised his hands.

"It may be easier than you think," he said. "Painless, in fact—if
you're lucky. We'll learn in a moment how farsighted you might
have been."

As Ryle's hands began moving, Pol fought down the desire to
strike back. A small voice seemed to be saying, "Not yet." Per-

haps it was himself. He shifted his vision to the second seeing and saw a great orange wave rolling toward him.

When it struck, he felt a certain slowing and then a rigidity of his thought processes. A genuine stiffness came over his body. Gone was any certainty as to what he wanted or did not want.

Ryle was speaking and his voice seemed somehow more distant than their proximity indicated:

"What is your name?"

It was with a peculiar fascination that he felt his lips move, heard his own voice reply, "Pol Detson."

"By what name were you known in the world where you grew up?"

"Daniel Chain."

"Do you possess the seven statuettes that are the Keys to the Gate?"

Suddenly, a sheet of flame hung between them. Ryle did not seem aware of its presence.

"No," Pol heard himself reply.

The fat sorcerer looked puzzled. Then he smiled.

"That was awkwardly phrased," he said, almost apologetically. "Can you tell me the location or locations of the seven magical statuettes which once belonged to your father?"

"No," Pol answered.

"Why not?" Ryle asked.

"I do not know where they are," Pol said.

"But you have seen them, handled them, had them in your possession?"

"Yes."

"What became of them?"

"They were stolen from me, on the way to Belken."

"I do not believe that."

Pol remained silent.

". . . But you are to be congratulated for your foresight," Ryle continued. "You have guarded against self-betrayal with a very powerful spell. It would take me a long time to ascertain its exact nature and to break it. Unfortunately for you, I have neither the time nor inclination, and you must be forced to speak. I have already mentioned the means which will be employed."

The man began another series of gestures, and Pol felt a certain clarity return to his consciousness. As this feeling grew, the image of the flame faded.

"I have also restored your appearance, for esthetic purposes,"

Ryle said. "Now that you are yourself again, is there anything that you would care to add to what you said?"

"No."

"I didn't think so."

The fat sorcerer turned away, crossed the room, opened the door.

"Larick?" he called.

"Yes?" came a distant voice.

"Take this man back to his cell," he said. "I'll send for him when the interrogation room has been made ready."

"You tried a coercion spell?"

"Yes. A good one. He's protected. We'll have to go the other route."

"A pity."

"Yes."

Ryle turned back.

"Pol, go along with him."

Pol moved, turning, advancing slowly toward the doorway. He wondered as he did . . . He would be passing very close to Ryle. If he were to turn suddenly and attack the man, he felt that he could deal with him fairly quickly, before the other could bring any magic into play. Then, of course, he would have to fight Larick, and he wondered whether he could dispatch Ryle before the younger sorcerer was upon him. For that matter . . .

A vision of the flame flashed before him again.

"Not yet," came the voice in his mind. "Wait. Soon. Restrain yourself."

Nodding mentally, he passed Ryle and stepped out into the corridor where Larick waited.

"All right," Larick said, and he commenced walking, heading in the opposite direction from which they had come.

Pol heard the door of the room he had quitted close behind him. One quick rabbit punch, he decided, just below that kerchief he always wears, and Larick will be out of the picture . . .

Almost predictably, the image of the flame passed before his eyes once again.

"Turn here."

He turned, then said, "This isn't the way we came."

"I know that, you son of a bitch. I want to show you what your kind have done."

Suddenly, they passed into a familiar area, and with a touch of panic Pol realized where they were headed and what it was that he was being taken to see. He slowed his pace.

"Come along. Come along."

No plan presented itself to him, but the pulse of power still throbbed in his disguised arm. He decided to rely upon the guidance of the invisible flame. Something would provide him with an opportunity, very soon, he felt, an opportunity to smash Larick and—

Of course. His future actions came into perfect focus. He was suddenly certain as to what was going to occur, knew exactly what he was going to do when it did.

They entered the cavern. Larick produced a magical light which traveled on before them, illuminating their advance. Pol readied himself as they made their way around to the place where the opened, empty casket lay. Just a few more steps . . .

He heard Larick cry out. The sounds echoed from the rocky walls. His vision swam through the second seeing. Bands of bright, colored light moved everywhere. When he tried, he was able to resolve them into strands, but the moment he relaxed this effort they became bands again—horizontal, not drifting, but moving slowly upward, of various widths. After a moment, he saw that they overlay a field of vertical bands, and beyond them, diagonals. The world had acquired a peculiarly cubist structure. And he realized in that instant that he had but shifted to another mode of seeing the same thing which had always been presented to him as the strands—and he knew that there were others beyond it and that, somehow, in the future, he would always view the magical world in the mode most appropriate to his needs of the moment rather than the more restricted vision his power had brought him in the past. And he knew, intuitively, how to use these bands just as he had known in the past what the strands were for. It took a great effort to restrain himself from reaching out to manipulate them as Larick turned toward him, teeth bared.

"She's gone!" he said. "Stolen! How—?"

Then his eyes took on a strange cast and his head slowly turned to his right. Pol was certain that he, too, was now into the second seeing and something in his version of it was indicating to him the direction in which Taisa had been taken.

Larick turned suddenly and moved rapidly, heading off along the ledge. The light which had guided them remained stationary, somewhere behind Pol, spilling its pale light into the empty casket.

Pol advanced, moving onto the ledge, holding his second sight in focus, ready to utilize his new understanding of magical processes. He hurried toward the natural light at the end of the tunnel, rushing past the place where he had hidden the statuette.

When he came into the chamber, a chorus of voices burst upon his consciousness: "Now! Now! Now! Now! Now! Now! Now!"

Larick, his back to him, was bent over Taisa's still form upon the sacrificial stone, perhaps ten paces before him. Pol reached up with both hands and seized upon an orange band, feeling his will go forth through the dragonmark.

In a moment, it was loose and swinging freely, like a long, bright pole, sweeping toward Larick.

Even as he made the gesture, however, Pol saw Larick stiffen and begin to turn, knowing that the other sorcerer had heard the sounds of his entrance. He saw the look of astonishment upon his face, succeeded immediately by one of apprehension.

But Larick managed to move, and he moved quickly. His left hand shot upward, fingers knotting. He seized upon a red diagonal and jerked it into the path of Pol's attack.

The force of the blow knocked him sprawling upon the floor, but he had managed to keep it from striking him. Pol turned the long shaft which he still held, and with a chopping motion of his left hand shortened it to a javelin. Larick shook his head and began pushing himself up from the floor. His gaze locked with Pol's as Pol was drawing back his right arm to hurl the gleaming shaft.

Larick pushed himself back onto his heels and raised both arms high up over his head. Pol cast the spear of light directly toward him and Larick dropped his arms. The bright bands which lay before him jumped and seemed to turn on their longitudinal axes.

It was like the sudden snapping shut of a Venetian blind. Larick was momentarily invisible behind a rainbow wall. Pol's lance struck against it and both the shaft and the wall seemed to shatter in a fountain of sparks. As these fell away, he saw Larick standing, moving his hands cross-body.

His peripheral vision warned him, barely in time. Larick was operating two lateral diagonals like a bright pair of scissors. Pol extended both hands before him and rushed forward.

He seized upon a vertical and thrust it before him into the jaws of the light-spell. The diagonals closed upon it, their edges halting inches from his waist. He saw a slight sign of strain upon Larick's face as the man's hands tightened further. The diagonals jerked

©JUDY KING RIENIETS 81

nearer. He pushed even harder himself, holding them back. Larick leaned forward, straining against the pressure.

Abruptly, Pol heaved forward with all of his strength, throwing himself backward, dropping to the floor and rolling to the side as Larick staggered back and the bands closed above him.

Regaining his feet, he faced Larick again, watching his hands. He began circling the other at a distance of about fifteen feet and Larick turned slowly, accommodating his position to the movement. Slowly, the other sorcerer's hands began to move in an elaborate pattern. Pol followed them as closely as he could but was unable to detect any manipulation of the magical materials as he now perceived them.

Suddenly, Larick's foot passed through a wide, sweeping gesture and one of the lower bands took Pol across the ankles and he pitched sideways to the floor. Cursing himself for being misdirected so easily, he struggled to rise.

But the floor seemed to ripple and heave, preventing his recovery. As he fought against it, he realized that his weight no longer rested upon the floor, but that he now rode upon a rippling wave of the bands several inches above it. It was then that he began to realize that technique in these matters could be more important than raw energy. He could not regain his footing, but supported himself on his knees and left hand. He saw Larick's right foot moving rapidly up and down as if pumping a piano pedal, keeping the surface in agitation beneath him. It seemed that Larick's facility so far exceeded his that effective counter-measures were a matter of reflex to him, whereas Pol had to think for several moments to decide upon each attack and defense.

He wondered then whether a magical attack was the ultimate answer in dealing with the man. If he could only get near enough to land a blow capable of distracting Larick from magical manipulations, he felt confident that his own boxer's reflexes would be sufficient to deal with him in hand to hand fighting. If they were not, then he'd a feeling that he'd simply met a better man . . .

The bands! They could obviously be employed to support one's weight. So . . .

Reaching upward, he took hold of the higher, rising bands and drew himself upright, continuing the motion until he swung free above the heaving layer. Larick's right hand was already moving, out to the side, at shoulder level.

Pol reached far forward, took hold of another horizontal, swung upon it, directly toward Larick.

He was able to twist his body aside at the last possible moment, release himself and drop.

Larick had held a three-foot blade of green light, sword-like, swung ready to impale him.

He felt the normal floor beneath him again, and he snatched at a diagonal band of yellow light, willing it into blade-form, dragging it into an *en garde* position as he struggled for footing. It was the first time in this world that he had held anything like a blade in his hands—and also the first time since the end of the previous fencing season at the university.

He parried a head cut and leaped backward, not having sufficient footing and balance to venture a riposte. As he recovered and Larick advanced, he became aware of two things simultaneously: Larick was facing him full-body rather than sidewise, and a dark oblong several feet in length had taken form upon his left arm.

He backed away as Larick came on. Blade and shield was not normal collegiate fencing. It was something medieval—slower, more ponderous, entailing different footwork. He was not about to materialize a shield of his own and face Larick on terms with which the other man had to be more familiar.

Larick swung his blade through a chest cut and Pol leaped backward, entirely avoiding any engagement. Larick continued his advance, Pol his retreat.

Quickly, he reviewed everything he knew concerning the other's techniques. Larick should be unfamiliar with the lunge; also, most of his bladework should involve the edge rather than the point of the weapon. Pol maintained a saber en garde, but began thinking in terms of the épée.

He halted his retreat and feinted a chest cut. Larick raised his shield slightly and moved to ready his blade for a slashing riposte. Pol did not follow through, and he saw that Larick was beginning to smile.

He adopted a low stance and beat once upon the other's blade. The attack followed.

The moment Larick's blade moved, Pol was back and up, very straight and high, his weapon describing a clockwise semicircle into an overhand position, from which he executed a stop-thrust to the other's forearm. Larick made a small noise in his throat as Pol then continued the movement through a full bind in anticipation of going in for the body past the edge of the shield.

But the weapon spun out of Larick's hand, and he stepped

backward, covering himself more fully. Pol smiled, stamped his foot and rushed him.

Larick raised his right arm, but Pol ignored it and threw a head-cut. The green blade came flying back from the floor into Larick's hand, and he parried it. Pol could not check his momentum, so he increased it, crashing into Larick's shield before he could riposte.

As Larick staggered back, Pol chopped heavily at his weapon, knocking it aside, then kicked as hard as he could squarely against the center of the shield. Larick stumbled and Pol chopped again, knocking the blade from his hand once more. The shield swung aside and Pol was no longer in any orthodox fencing posture, but was near enough to drive his left fist into the other's midsection.

The shield fell away as he struck, and he cast his own weapon aside to throw a right at Larick's jaw.

Larick recovered, and raising his hands before his face, his elbows together over his midsection, rushed directly toward him. Pol stepped to the side and threw a left toward his head but did not connect.

Larick dropped and seized him about the knees. Pol felt himself go off balance, grabbed for Larick's shoulder, caught only a handful of his shirt and fell backward to the accompaniment of a tearing sound.

"Kill him! Hurry!" the voice came into his head.

As Pol fell, Larick attempted to hurl himself upon him but was met with a crosscut that knocked him off to the side. At that instant, Pol knew exactly what he must do.

He raised his right hand to shoulder level, palm upward, as he rolled to straddle Larick's supine form. His dragonmark throbbed as the blackness of the lines which separated the bands about him fled toward his hand and coalesced into a dark ball of negation, cancellation, death.

As he swung the ball downward toward Larick's face, his eyes jerked once and he barely had time to twist his body and hurl the death-sphere across the room, away.

Larick struggled to rise, and he clipped him once, hard, on the point of the chin and felt him grow slack. Then he rocked back onto his heels, brushed his hair out of his eyes and stared.

He reached slowly forward. There, where he had torn away the sleeve . . . Larick's right arm lay bare.

His hand trembled slightly as he touched the exposed dragon-mark above Larick's right wrist.

XVI.

Ryle Merson's voice filled the chamber:

"Is he still alive?"

Pol ignored it, reached up and removed the bandana from Larick's head. A single streak of white ran through his dark hair, front to back.

Only then did Pol turn his head and regard the heavy figure which had just come into the chamber.

"Have you slain him?" Ryle asked.

Pol stood and took a step toward the man.

"I haven't killed anyone here, yet," he said. "Who is Larick, anyway? And what is he to you?"

"How did you come free of the spell which bound you?"

"No. You answer me. I want to know about Larick."

"How quickly you forget your position," Ryle said softly. "You may have freed yourself from direct control, but your leash is short."

He spoke then the words which dissolved the spell of illusion, and the human guise slipped from Pol to reveal the monster body.

"The spell stands ready for the final transfer of which I spoke," he said, "requiring but the proper guide-word."

"I think not," Pol replied, and his will flowed forth through the dragonmark, shattering the image of the monstrous form which hung over him; his features flowed back into their normal pattern, and his hair was stirred as by an invisible wind, its natural color returning, the white streak reappearing.

His garments hung in rags upon him and he breathed heavily for several moments, but he smiled.

"Answer me now," he said. "Who is Larick?"

Ryle's face grew pale.

"Back when your father and I were still on friendly terms," he said, "he gave his young son into my care, as an apprentice."

"Larick is my brother?"

Ryle nodded.

"He is about five years older than you."

"What have you done to him?"

"I taught him the Art and I raised him to be a good man, to respect the decent things—"

Pol did a quick calculation.

"He was perfect insurance, too—when you broke with my father —wasn't he? You had a hostage then, against the wrath of your former friend."

"I am not ashamed to admit it," Ryle replied. "You never knew your father. The man was a devil. And he was one of the best sorcerers around. I had to have some protection."

A sudden flash of inspiration possessed him and Pol asked, "Could it be that Spier, who was still on good terms with my father, did what he did to your daughter in order to assure Larick's safety?"

The color returned heavily to Ryle's face.

"You think just like them, don't you?" he said. "Yes. Even your father hadn't pierced my defenses, but that bastard got through and did that thing to her. Larick has felt guilty about it all his life."

"With no small help from you, I'd guess. That's how you keep him in line, huh? The old guilt trip?"

"Something you've never felt, I'm sure. You're ready to cut a helpless girl's throat. You'd have done it by now if I hadn't heard Larick's cry."

"I'd rather cut yours," Pol said, moving forward. "You're a damned hypocrite. You're no better than my father or Spier. Maybe you're worse. You were ready to go along with their plan when you thought there was something in it for you. When you saw you had something to lose you became a white magician and a defender of righteousness. It's a lot of bullshit! You haven't changed. Now you make my brother do your dirty work, to keep your own hands clean. But they're not. You're not a big enough fool to believe they are, are you?"

Ryle moved his hands into the beginning of a warding gesture, and Pol slipped immediately into the second seeing, dragonmark still pounding with his pulsebeat.

"You talk to me of morality when you hold the Keys to the Gate and my daughter lies ready for your blade? Who is the hypocrite, Detson?"

An arc of fire passed between the man's fingertips, and Pol looked about for strands or bands, in vain.

But then, suddenly, it seemed as if great clouds of colored fog were drifting into the chamber.

Pol extended his hand and a blue mist was there when he needed it. He felt the condensing moisture upon his fingers. A moment later, he passed a globe of water the size of a basketball, dripping, from hand to hand. Fire. Water. It seemed he had the logical remedy ready for whatever Ryle had in mind.

As he waited for the older sorcerer to make the first move, he thought back over his battles with Keth and with Larick, wondering again why his perception of the magical world had altered in each instance. Then it occurred to him that on each occasion his vision could have been colored by the other's magical world-view. Perhaps, now, Ryle's world was somewhat more cloudy than most.

"We change each other's way of seeing, don't we?" he said, half-aloud.

"I am here to kill you, not to instruct you," Ryle replied, and the fires he held became a curved dagger which he cast toward Pol's breast.

Pol willed coldness and felt it flow through his fingertips. The watery sphere clouded and grew solid, covered with frost. The blade gouged ice chips from it when it struck, and then fell to the floor. Pol hurled the ice ball at Ryle, but the sorcerer stepped aside and it shattered against the wall behind him.

Ryle raised both arms and lowered them suddenly. The room vanished. They inhabited a region composed entirely of themselves and the colored clouds. Pol took another step forward. As before, he reasoned that if he could get within striking distance with his fists he could become a sufficient distraction to dispense with the magic and then, of course, with Ryle.

He moved to take another step forward and his way was blocked by the abrupt appearance of a low wall. He began to step over it and its top was suddenly studded with tall shards of glass. He withdrew and bumped against something. Glancing quickly to the rear, he beheld another wall. And then there was one to his right, and his left. Almost simultaneous with his awareness of their existence, they began to move nearer. Ryle was staring intently toward him, the palms of his hands facing one another and moving slowly together.

But there was no up, no down here. He willed the fogs to boil beneath him, to levitate him as the bands had done earlier.

He rose out of his prison then and passed over its forward wall. It seemed almost too easy . . .

© JUDY KING RIENIETS 81

Studying Ryle then, he saw traces of concern about those prob-
ing eyes. The man did not know his strengths or his weaknesses
yet, knew only what he had accomplished thus far. And so there
was fear. So he was fighting a very conservative duel at this point,
testing him, watching him, keeping his distance. Such seeming the
case, Pol was suddenly apprehensive himself. Ryle was doubtless
very good at this sort of thing. In a little while he would realize
the limits of Pol's experience and would likely unleash a devastat-
ing attack. Pol was not at all certain that he could survive it.
Therefore, he ought to act quickly and decisively. But how? He
could not think of an appropriate offense in this silent, dreamlike
place of deadly cotton candy. Unless . . .

Perhaps he might change the rules, change the milieu. Perhaps
he had, in some fashion, been guilty of letting the other man
choose his own battleground. There was so much that he still did
not know . . .

He felt that he had to finish with Ryle as quickly as possible.
Beyond the possibility of Larick's recovering at any time and coming to the aid of his adversary, Pol feared a recurrence of the
effect he had already experienced several times—that unpredictable, intermittent failing of his powers.

He had wondered several times since he had fought Keth
whether all of the symbolic byplay was truly necessary in a magical encounter. Since it was will against will, force manipulation
against force manipulation and, perhaps, personal energy against
personal energy, it would seem that it might be stripped to its
barest essentials and Devil take the hindmost. It occurred to him
immediately that this was an untutored, Madwand way of thinking. But he was slowed whenever he tried to imitate the refine-
ments the others had developed in the long courses of their stud-
ies, and he knew that he was handicapped when he was forced to
play their games. There were obvious advantages in doing things
that more subtle way, but he had no time to learn it at the moment. Therefore, he determined to attempt the alternative as he
tried to move nearer.

With some trepidation, he blanked the second seeing. The fogs
vanished. The room returned to normal, Ryle standing near its entrance, a faraway look in his eyes.

Pol raised his right hand, directing it toward Ryle, and willed
that the other fall down, shrivel and die. The dragonmark seemed
suddenly icy and he felt the power leap forth. He continued to

focus his will and a steady flowing sensation moved, wavelike, down his arm.

Ryle swayed for a moment, then steadied himself. Suddenly, Pol found himself standing on a spit of land, his stance unaltered, a mighty torrent of water rushing past him at either hand. Ryle stood upon a small island downstream. Even as he watched, the nearer edge of Ryle's islet was being eroded away and the man was forced to draw back upon it.

But Ryle raised both hands, a look of intense concentration upon his face. The movement of the water began to slow. A tremor shook the land upon which Pol stood. The water lashed about for several moments, then grew still. This did not last long, however. Shortly, it began moving again. But this time it was flowing toward Pol. He watched, fascinated, as its velocity increased and the land began to wear away before him.

He shook his head as if to clear it. Ryle had drawn him back into a symbolic situation. He dismissed the waters for a moment and bent his efforts toward reestablishing his presence in the chamber.

The river vanished. They were back in the room again. Nothing had changed. Only now Pol felt a pressure, a pronounced squeezing sensation all over his body. It was increasing by the moment.

He refocussed his energies.

"Burn, melt, fall down . . ."

The pressure vanished and Ryle staggered, as from a sudden blow. Pol maintained his own pressure now, his entire will behind it. Ryle began to sway, as if caught in a heavy wind.

Then, suddenly, there were flames between them, fanned as if by a great gale blowing in Ryle's direction. They rose from a wide chasm which divided a rocky landscape between them.

Even as he watched, the winds died down and the flames became vertical. Then he felt the warm touch of a breeze upon his face. The tongues of fire began to bend toward him . . .

"No!" Pol cried, and the vista was swept away.

The breeze and the heat remained until he gained control of his forces once again. Then they fell, and he hurled his energies at the other with renewed vehemence.

. . . He stood upon a mountain peak, Ryle atop another. A storm was raging between them. Bolts of lightning fell upon both slopes—

"No," he said softly, "not this time," and he stood again in the chamber and continued the pressure.

. . . Each of them stood upon a floe of ice, tossed by a gray, choppy sea—

"No."

They were in the chamber and Ryle was glaring at him. His arm was beginning to ache, but the wavelike sensation continued to pulse through it.

. . . There was darkness all about them, and the meteor shower began—

"No."

He maintained the focus of his concentration, ready to dismiss any new distraction. It had to be will against will.

The room began to fade and he restored it immediately.

"No."

He smiled.

For half a minute he maintained his assault, and then he felt the pressure beginning to mount against him. He drew upon his reserves of determination, but it continued to build.

Even this way, he realized then, Ryle had the edge. The man had played a careful game but it had not really been necessary. He knew that he could not hold him back much longer. Ryle really was stronger. Of course, he had no way of knowing that.

Pol took another step forward. If he could just reach him, could just use his fists again . . .

But the pressure grew excruciating with the next step. He knew that he would never make it across the chamber. And now the fat sorcerer was beginning to smile . . .

"Father?"

Ryle turned his head and the pressure was gone. Off to his left, Pol could see that Taisa was sitting up upon the slab of stone.

"Taisa . . . ?"

The man took a step forward.

Pol gathered his forces and struck. Ryle fell like a poled ox.

"Father!"

Taisa slumped back upon the stone. Larick, who had been stirring, grew still.

Gargantuan peals of laughter shook the room.

XVII.

The wolf paced and turned in the great cavern, below the Face, before the frozen forms of the other beasts and the men. He slipped out only briefly to find something to eat, unable to go too great a distance from the lair, and a part of his mind always kept watch upon the entrance. He made his kill quickly and took it back with him into the grotto. He lay before the shadowy forms of the other hosts, crunching bones. Beyond this, there was only silence.

When he rose again, his movements were less rapid and they continued to slow, as did his heartbeat and his breathing.

Finally, he was barely stirring, and at last he came to a halt. His eyes grew glazed. He became totally immobile.

Slowly then, a serpent uncoiled itself upon a ledge near the place of the Face. It twisted its way down the rough, rocky wall, tongue darting, eyes bright. It slithered across the floor. It fell upon the remains of the wolf's meal and consumed them.

It mounted the wall again, exploring ledge after ledge, entering each cranny and crack, eating any insects it came upon. Tongue darting, it tested every stirring of the air.

Hours passed, its movements slowed. At length, it stopped within a night-dark crevice.

The big cat awakened and stretched. She went to regard the still and expressionless Face high upon the wall. She patrolled the cavern. She left briefly to feed, as the wolf had done, returned and grew stiff as she licked her rectum, one leg high overhead.

A man awakened. He cursed, drew his blade and inspected it, sheathed it. He began to pace. After a time, he spoke to the Face. It never replied, but he was not misled. He could feel the intelligence, the power within it. The sightless eyes seemed to follow him wherever he went.

At last his words trailed off and he became a part of the scenery.

The Harpy awakened and uttered a cry and a curse. She flapped in quick patrol about the cavern, defecating profusely, imaginatively.

Then she considered the Face and grew silent. She went to feed at the remains of the cat's meal.

All were as one before the Face.

XVIII.

Pol turned toward the doorway. An unnaturally cast shadow covered the large figure of the man who stood there. As soon as Pol's gaze fell upon him, that one moved forward and entered the chamber. The shadow went away.

Pol stared. The man wore a yellow cloak, darker garments beneath it. He was blue-eyed, with sandy hair white at the temples. His features were rugged, his expression almost open, almost honest. He smiled. He had a shiny, capped tooth.

"There is a lesson there for you, lad," he said, and Pol recognized the voice. "He had you, but he allowed himself to be distracted. I lifted an old spell, to give you an opening, to see what you would do." He shook his head. "You shouldn't have allowed yourself to be distracted, also. You should have struck instantly, not stood gawking. A better man could have killed you in that interval—would have."

"But the distraction itself might have represented a threat," Pol replied.

"If a building is falling on you, you don't concern yourself with the horn of an approaching car. You deal with the most immediate peril first. That's survival. You were good, but you hesitated. That can be fatal."

"Car? Who the hell are you, anyway?"

"You know my name."

"Henry Spier?"

The man smiled again.

"So much for introductions."

From somewhere, he produced a black cigarette holder, screwed a cigarette into it and raised it to his lips. Smoke drifted upward from it before it reached his mouth. He puffed upon it and looked about the chamber.

"Things seem to have worked themselves out just about as I'd calculated them," he observed.

He reached beneath his cloak and produced the statuette Pol had hidden in the tunnel.

"You found it . . ."

"Of course."

Henry Spier walked past him and placed the figure at the second point from the right in the diagram upon the floor.

"Six to go," he commented as he straightened and turned.

"That is the first cigarette I've seen in this world," Pol said.

"A man of perception may choose his pleasures from many places," Spier replied. "I'll be happy to teach you all about them later. But now we have some important business to conclude."

"My dreams," Pol said. "You released me from what I might call the first series, that night on the trail . . ."

Spier nodded.

". . . But then there were more—set in the same world, but very different."

Again Spier nodded, and the smoke curled above his head.

"Since you were being propagandized in the first instance," he stated, "I felt it only fair that you should be granted a somewhat fuller picture when the opposition had its opportunity."

"I must confess that the fuller picture was not entirely comprehensible to me."

"It would be surprising if it were," said Spier, "since it was an alien and vastly older civilization that you viewed. What is far more important, though, is whether or not you found it attractive."

Spier's eyes suddenly met with his own and Pol looked away.

"I found it—fascinating," he said, and when he looked back he saw that Spier was smiling again.

"Excellent," the man replied. "I believe that finds us in basic agreement as to values. What say you produce the other six Keys now and we be about our business?"

Pol looked about the chamber. He gestured.

"You cautioned me against inattention and distraction. What of these?"

"My power would have to be broken for these three to awaken," he said. "It would require a faltering of my will, and I doubt the sufficiency of anything I propose doing now to work that end."

Pol shook his head and turned away. He regarded the still form of Taisa upon the block of dark stone.

"Your gaze follows the direction of your thoughts, I see."

"Does this thing really require a human sacrifice?"

"Yes. So be of good cheer that you now have a choice. We can save the girl for your later pleasure and use Ryle, who would be most happy to kill you if it would serve his ends."

"What of—my brother?"

"He would not go along with our plans. Ryle has warped his thinking. I suggest you permit me to banish him, perhaps to the world where you yourself grew up."

"He is a sorcerer. He may find his way back."

"It will be a simple enough matter to inflict a loss of memory."

"That could be kind of rough."

"His treatment of you was somewhat less than exemplary."

"But as you said, Ryle influenced him."

"Who cares what the reason may be? I am only willing to spare him at all because he *is* your brother."

"Say that I give you what you want. What assurance have I that I will be of any use to you afterwards?"

"There will be massive changes, and I cannot control an entire world by myself. There are not that many Madwands about. I would not dispense with any of them unnecessarily. And you, of course, will always hold a special place, because of this assistance."

"I see," Pol said.

"Do you really? Are you aware what will come to pass in this world when the Gate is opened?"

"I think so. Or at least I have my suspicions."

"It will become our plum. With the power at our disposal, we will be gods of the new world."

Pol's eyes moved toward the Gate, where some trick of the light made the figure of the nailed bird seem to jerk forward.

"Supposing I said 'no'?" he asked.

"That could cause us both considerable inconvenience. But what possible reason could you have for not agreeing?"

"I don't like being pressured into things, whether it's by you or Ryle or the statuettes themselves. I've been manipulated ever since I set foot in this world, and I'm tired of it."

"Well, as in most major matters there is only a limited number of choices. In this case, you are with me, you are against me or you want to walk away from me. Two of those responses are unacceptable and would require action on my part."

"I wouldn't like that," said Pol. "But then, you might not either."

"Are you threatening me, lad?" Spier asked.

"Just stating a possible consequence," Pol replied.

The big man sighed.

"You're strong, Pol," he said, "stronger today than you ever were before in your life. You've passed your initiation, and your lights are all shining as pretty as can be—for the moment. No telling how long it will last, of course. But be that as it may, I am stronger still. There would be no contest whatsoever between us. You would be as a candle's flame before the hurricane of my will. Now, I could force you to produce the Keys. But I would far rather you did it willingly, for I want you alive and on my side and wearing no special enchantment."

"Why?"

"I've my reasons. I'll tell you later, after I'm sure of you."

"You foresaw a possible conflict between us. Something you'd said . . ."

"Yes, I did. But it need not be. If you're squeamish, I'll even do the sacrificing myself."

Pol laughed.

"That's not it. I'd have killed Ryle only a little while ago if I could have. As I said, you're pressing me, you're manipulating me."

"I have no choice."

"The hell you don't."

Spier turned away, staring for a moment at the Gate.

"I wonder . . . ?" he began.

"By the way," Pol said, "if you were to kill me, how would you get at the Keys?"

"Only with great difficulty, if at all," Spier said, "since you are carrying them around in what is practically a private universe. If you die, it would be a hell of a problem piercing it."

"Then your candle in the wind metaphor isn't quite apt, is it? You'd have to pull your punches if it came to throwing any."

"Perhaps. Perhaps not. I wouldn't count on it, though. The Gate could be opened with just one Key—but it might take me a couple of years and an awful lot of trouble. Good thing we're just speaking hypothetically, isn't it?"

Pol crossed the chamber and touched the Gate for the first time. It felt cold. The eyes of the nailed serpent seemed to be fixed upon him.

"What would happen if the statuettes were destroyed?" he asked.

"That would be a very difficult thing to accomplish," Spier replied, "even if one knew how."

"But we're being hypothetical, aren't we?"

"True. The Gate would fade away from this plane, and you would be standing there looking at a raw piece of mountain."

"But it is open now—or can be opened without the Keys—on another plane?"

"Yes. But only tenuous things can take that route, as you did in your dreams."

"What brought it here in the first place?"

"Your father, Ryle and myself—with great exertions."

"How? And how are the statuettes involved?"

"That's enough for being hypothetical—or anything else of an interrogatory nature," Spier said. "There were three choices—one good one and two bad ones. Do you recall?"

"Yes."

Pol turned toward him, leaned back against the door and folded his arms across his breast. Immediately, he felt the coldness along his spine, but he did not move. The power was still there, moving within his right forearm.

Spier's eyes widened, slightly and but for an instant. He glanced upward and then back down at Pol again.

"I know your answer," he said, "but I have to hear you say it."

"You ran out on my father and left him to face an army."

Spier frowned, looked puzzled.

"He acted against my advice," he said. "The army was there because of his actions, not mine. There was no sense in my dying with him. But what is all of this to you? You never even knew him."

"Just curious," Pol said. "I wanted to hear your side of it."

"Surely you are not going to use that as a basis for refusing me? You were only a baby."

Pol nodded. He was thinking of the thing that might have been his father's ghost walking beside him in the misty chamber.

"You're right. But humor me with one more question, if you will. Would the two of you have fought one another eventually, for hegemony in this new land?"

Spier's face reddened.

"I don't know," he said. "Perhaps . . ."

"Had it already begun? Were you on the threshold and was this your way—"

"Enough!" Spier cried. "I take it that your answer is 'no'.

Would you care to tell me which is your real reason for denying me?"

Pol shrugged.

"Choose any of the above," he said. "Maybe I'm not certain myself. But I know there is a sufficiency."

The coldness had invaded his entire body now, but he made no move to withdraw from the serpent figure of the Gate against which he leaned. It was almost as if it had invited him to position himself just there . . .

"It's a shame," Spier said, "because I was beginning to like you . . ."

Pol hit him. He summoned up every bit of the power he could muster, backed it with all of his will and hurled it at the man.

Very slowly, Henry Spier unscrewed the cigarette from its holder, dropped it upon the floor and stepped on it. He replaced the holder in some hidden pocket beneath his cloak. It had to be sheer bravado. Pol knew that the man must be feeling the force of his attack. But the display was effective. Pol felt a tremor of fear at Spier's power, but he maintained the siege and reached for even more force to back it. He was committed now, and he felt as if he were sliding down a long tunnel which ended in blackness.

Spier raised his eyes and they bored into his own. Pol suddenly felt a resistance rising.

Spier took a step toward him.

It was as if he suddenly faced a heat backlash, as if the target of his exertions stood directly before him rather than some distance away.

Frantically, he switched to the second seeing. His vision focussed upon Spier, advancing upon him, fists raised. The image of Spier, still standing in the distance, faded. The man's face was twisted into a smirk and perspiration dotted his brow. His fist was already moving.

Pol's concentration was broken. He ducked forward, raising his hands to protect his face. He heard a solid *thunk,* followed by a brief cry and realized immediately that Spier's blow had fallen upon the Gate.

He dropped his hands and drove his left fist, followed by his right, into Spier's abdomen. The blows had surprisingly little effect. The man was solid.

Even as he swung a left uppercut and felt it connect, he realized that the main pain the man seemed to have felt was in the bloodied knuckles of his right hand, which he now held in an awkward position. Pol immediately threw a right toward his face, but this blow was blocked. Then Spier rushed him.

Spier's bulk crashed into him, driving him back against the Gate. Pol was dazed as his head struck upon it. Then Spier stepped back and their eyes met again.

He called upon the dragonmark to raise a defense as a shock ran through his entire system like a jolt of electricity. He struck out with the power he had wielded earlier, but it barely seemed to shield him against the forces the other was turning against him. He felt a pressure beginning to build, not unlike that which Ryle had turned upon him. Both he and Spier stood absolutely still now, and though he threw everything he had into the defense, the pressure continued to mount.

A throbbing began in his temples and his breathing became labored. He grew damp with perspiration, though he still felt abnormally cold. A wave of dizziness came and went, came again. He felt that he might only be able to hold Spier off for a few more seconds. His defenses would crumble, the man would place him under control, force him to produce the statuettes and then possibly use him for the sacrifice. Where was the flame which had guided him, protected him?

He seemed to hear faint, mocking laughter. In that instant he realized that this was the end toward which they had guided him. They wanted the Gate opened. If he were not willing, then they would not protect him against the one who would.

His vision began to fade as the vertigo returned. If this were to be the end, then at least he ought to try inflicting a final hurt upon his enemy.

He placed his right foot flat upon the door behind him and thrust himself forward toward Spier, striking outward and upward with both fists.

He was surprised that his blow actually landed. The last thing that he saw before he fell was the look of astonishment on Spier's face as the man toppled over backwards.

A wave of darkness rushed through Pol's head. He felt nothing as he hit the floor.

XIX.

Drifting. He was drifting through blackness and silence. His only other sensation was a feeling of intense cold, but after a time this passed.

For how long he drifted, he could not tell—moments, ages . . . The sensation was not unpleasant, now that the coldness had passed. Memory required too much effort. He only knew that it was good to know something of rest, of an end to all exertion.

A gentle rocking motion began. Even so . . . It was hardly disturbing. But then motion commenced in a single direction. He rode with it, still feeling the rocking as he was drawn along.

He perceived a faint light. It seemed to be coming from all directions, but he did not wonder at the variety of sensory apparatus the sensation might require. His consciousness was growing, but portions of his mind were numb.

The light grew and the motion continued. Whatever was below seemed a pale yellow with smoky patches.

Now the prospect grew clearer, but his sense of perspective was warped. The light values were strange, and there was no way of determining his distance from the slowly resolving objects below. It was a broken land, rocky, sandy, shadowed, with wind-borne clouds of dust and low-lying, snaky mists. But there was nothing recognizable for contrast, nothing to provide a scale. Yet the place was familiar. Where? When?

He dropped lower. Were they mountain peaks or low ridges above which he moved?

And where was he going? Was he controlling his own movements, only drifting, or both? Or neither? It almost seemed—

He was moving alongside one of the larger stone prominences. Suddenly, he rounded it and the matter of relative proportions was resolved.

About ten feet below him, high on a stake, a demonic head was impaled. Something which might be classifiable as a grin drew the

dark, scaly face tight. The eyes were fully opened, very black and appeared to be staring directly at him.

He felt something akin to a shudder as he was swept on past the grisly thing, with the distinct impression that it had winked at him. The wasteland fell farther below him as he soared into a twilit area of pale stars in a pale sky above the level of blowing dust. Here the wind still blew, cold, with a moaning sound, empty of everything.

Far below now, the features of the landscape fled backward. A fountain of sparks rose as if to intercept him, but he veered far wide of it. Shortly afterwards, a crashing metallic note filled the air, as of the striking of a great gong, the reverberations of which seemed to remain with him for many long minutes.

A bright meteor cut a long, slow trail above and before him; and he heard a sound like thunder though there were no clouds in the sky. His velocity seemed to increase, and the moaning of the wind rose in pitch. Far below him, the dark and light patches of the land moved in a sea of distortions, rendering themselves into momentary faces—elongate, twisted, beautiful, alien, angry, composed, bereft. He passed over a shattered city above which dark forms hovered and turned. Small blue lights darted amid the ruins. Occasionally, the dark things fell upon one and extinguished it. He passed above a black tower from whence a lovely, liquid-voiced singing emerged. A squat, many-legged creature with a juicy, cracked skin, lay like a rotten plum atop it. A brazen chariot passed silently through the middle air, driven by a dead-white being muffled in saffron, drawn by long-tailed creatures whose breath emerged in white clouds to congeal and fall as crystals upon the winds. In a moment, the apparition was gone, and he began to doubt whether he had actually seen it.

A tinkling, as of hundreds of tiny bells, accompanied his passage above a gray plain where armies of humans and demons stood frozen in martial attitudes beneath some ancient enchantment whose fringes he had touched. Ahead of him then, the horizon was broken along its entire length—a thin, irregular edge of the world, rising. He focussed his attention upon it.

It grew into a saw-toothed band and then a rampart—mighty, towering and black. For a long while it seemed that at any moment he might be dashed against the great range. And then a shifting of light lay a new perspective across the land, and he realized that it was incredibly distant, incredibly huge. Something tightened within the cloud of his being as he realized intuitively that he must pass over it.

Below, the hidden features of the land were still revealed in fragmentary flashes. He no longer had vision to the rear, but he felt, vaguely, that something was following him. Briefly, he assaulted the frozen part of his own mind, with inquiry as to what he was, where he had come from. Nothing yielded, the brief frenzy passed and forgetfulness of its occurrence ensued. He continued his contemplation of the world before him, realizing that he had come this way before, knowing that this time it was different, knowing that he had a mission to fulfill.

The mountains loomed even larger, and he knew that—no matter what the nature of his form—their traversal would not be easy. He began studying their silhouette, looking for a low area, a gap— anything that might ease his passage. He thought that he detected such a place off to the left, and he made an effort to direct his course toward it.

He was surprised when this actually occurred. It was his first voluntary act that he could recall since coming into consciousness, and it pleased him to see it prove fruitful. Immediately, however, he wondered what had been directing him up until this time.

He became aware then of a kind of tugging, of the sensation of being drawn onward by something beyond the mountains, something which was willing to give him a little leeway, that he come more rapidly and safely into its lands. He exerted himself again, and his velocity increased.

As he drew nearer to the mountains it seemed that he grew more tangible than he had been earlier. For now he began to meet with resistance, to feel the buffeting of the winds.

The mountains towered above him, their peaks vanishing in the darkness overhead. He rose to an even greater altitude as he came nearer, approaching the gap. The winds caught him and cast him back down, screaming now in their passage.

He stabilized himself and mounted again, moving even nearer to the rocky face as he ascended. This time he rose higher before the screaming winds forced him back.

On his third attempt, he moved more rapidly, driving himself upward with great force, the slope of the mountain becoming a dark blur before him. When the winds finally took hold of him, he fought them, almost reaching the level of the bright gap before he was forced downward yet again.

The fourth time he tried a different angle of attack and was beaten back almost immediately.

He hovered at a lower altitude, recovering orientation and stability, mustering fortitude. He massed his energies once more. Then he began to rise.

This time he followed the best course he had taken earlier, close to the face of the mountain. He hurled himself upward, attempting to exceed all earlier velocities.

The wind curled about him and played upon him as on the string of some musical instrument. He throbbed to its vibrations as he fought it. He continued to rise against its pressures, but he felt the rapid dissipation of the energies which composed his being. A feeling came over him that if he did not make it up and through this time, he would be swept away to drift for perhaps half of an age before he recovered sufficient strength to try again.

As the battering increased and he felt himself slowing he invested all of his remaining strength in an attempt to continue the upward drive. A momentary lull permitted him a great gain, but the assault began again just as he neared the gap.

"Whoever you are that calls," he cried wordlessly toward the gap, "if you really want me, then lend a hand!"

Almost immediately, he felt the tugging—and for the first time it seemed a physical sensation rather than a psychical leading-on. He added his own energies to it and felt himself rising at a more rapid rate. He swept past the highest point he had achieved with his earlier efforts. The gap was before him if he could but bend his course and strike a proper passage now.

He exerted himself again, and the steady pull—from ahead now—assisted him. He came into the gap.

He had hoped for some sheltering from the winds once he achieved the cleft in the mountains, but now he faced a gale blowing through it. Fighting his way to the shelter of an opening in the righthand wall, he gathered his forces and considered the way ahead. He had seen prominences before him and other openings in the walls.

Braving the winds, he advanced and took shelter in the lee of a rocky rib to the left. The wind whistled by him and icy crystals sparkled in long streaks within dark grooves amid the stone. He made another effort, advancing a small distance and sheltering again. The tugging had subsided—or, rather, reverted to the mental level, as a summoning.

When he felt that he had regained sufficient strength, he entered the blast and moved forward once more. In such fashion, he traversed the long defile, finding himself at last in the final protected area, adjacent to the forward opening of the pass. As he waited there, he considered his course of action upon emerging. He decided to move immediately to the nearer side—this being the left—upon departing the gap, to prevent his being swept back into it.

As he traveled that final distance, he caught a glimpse of a dark and ancient sea, far ahead, before he slipped to the side, was taken by the winds and felt himself hurled skyward.

He rose at a rapid rate, and the world spun kaleidoscopically through whatever senses he possessed. He was tossed upward and outward away from the mountain and then found himself falling, to be caught and dragged through a washboard-like trough of turbulence. When this ended, he fell again, his senses in total disarray.

After a time, he slowed, and he became aware of the tugging once again. He drifted away from the region of high winds, continuing to lose altitude. Gradually, what passed for vision reasserted itself.

Below him, sweeping down to the still sea and seeming to continue beneath its surface, was a fantastic, terraced city of asymmetrical buildings, many of them of a darkly burnished metal, extending on to the right and the left to vanish at the horizon. He was drawn nearer to this place. Towers of colored smoke redolent with heavy perfumes drifted by him. His vision was constantly tricked by the unusual perspectives, the pale light. He drifted lower and saw where demons walked with their human lovers; he heard the strange, slow music from the revolving pentagons. He moved above an avenue lined with grotesque statues, all of them turning slowly in a centuries-long figure-dance. An enormous being, chained among russet pillars, wept continually into a stone basin from which green chalices were filled by the passers-by. Faint flashes like heat lightning colored the somber sky far out over the sea. He grew dizzy at the prospect; there was something new and not quite comprehensible in every direction that he looked. Such as the high, yellow tower near the seaside with the statue of the dark woman-like bird-thing crouched atop it . . .

Then it stirred and he knew that it was no statue.

Nyalith's voice went forth like trumpets across the land and the sea.

All motion below him was frozen for an instant.

And he knew.

He turned toward the waters and directed his course out over them, his velocity mounting steadily, the world becoming a gray, tunnel-like blur about him. He moved along that line of force which had drawn him across the world. He felt, for the first time, the presence toward which his flight was bearing him.

Before him, there occurred a darkness at the end of the tunnel. Then, for one flashing moment, he caught sight of the great black-winged form, limned against a violet sky, lightnings flickering about it. A moment only, and then he was swept to that destined rendezvous, his newly awakened consciousness shifting and breaking apart, merging.

He opened his beak and sent forth his answering cry across the still waters, a cry of exultation in the knowledge that he, Henry Spier, had been joined with the ancient consciousness of Prodromolu, Opener of the Way.

He rode the winds to a great height, then dived down to regard his own reflection in the waters—shadowy bird-form haloed in baleful light. Here was the power, he knew. He would summon his people and lead them across the land to the place of the Gate. There he would arouse his human body on the other side. It mattered not that but one Key was in place. This would prove sufficient with the Opener of the Way as aid, once the blood of any of the fallen was added to the spell. There was nothing now to stay the merger of the planes, the salvation of his world. He beat downward once with his wings, feeling their strength, grazing the surface of the water beneath which bright things moved.

Then, sea-splitting tower of scale and mud, it rose before him, red eyes unwinking, wrack of the depths adorning its horns, upon whose back the rock-shelled scavengers danced among skeletons of ships and shards of dead things' bones. And even as it reared, it swayed, the dragger-back-into-the-mud of primordial creation, Talkne, Serpent of the Still Waters, who had for eons awaited this passage and the renewal of their eternal conflict.

Prodromolu's wings went wide, scooping at the air, slowing his forward progress. In that instant before recovery, Talkne struck.

Hammerlike, the head of the serpent fell against the fluttering bird, driving it down among the waves amid a flurry of feathers. Talkne plunged after him.

Prodromolu's talons extended like switchblade scimitars, to gouge long furrows in the serpent's side. His beak slashed as Talkne threw a coil over his back.

Then they were rolling over and over in the water, sending up

mighty showers of spray, their blood darkening the foam as it billowed in all directions. His talons continued to slash against the side of the snake, seeking purchase there, as the coil tightened across his back and Talkne's head darted from side to side, moved forward, moved backward, seeking an opening for a deadly strike. Above them, the skies darkened and lightened again. Far across the water, the cry of Nyalith was repeated.

"It is a summons you will never answer, Bird," hissed Talkne.

"We've had this conversation before, Snake," Prodromolu answered.

For the first time, their eyes met, and both stared for a long, peculiar moment.

"Pol?" the bird croaked.

"Henry . . . ?"

And then Prodromolu struck, overwhelming the slower, human personality within. Talkne writhed in the sudden spasm of his talons, but the dark wings were already shrugging water as they beat with a sound like wet sails aluff, and the serpent was rolled onto her back, tail thrashing, as Prodromolu mounted the air and strove to raise the other into his own element.

Talkne fought back, heaving coil after coil toward the bird. But Prodromolu avoided them or slashed with his beak, never missing a beat with his pinions as he commenced a slow movement in the direction of the land, dragging the serpent after him, half-in, half-out of the water.

The bird uttered a triumphant cry as his velocity increased and more and more of Talkne's bulk was drawn into the air, dangling and writhing. After a time, the mountains came into view, and the world-city upon their slopes. It was then that the serpent struck again.

Talkne's head flashed upward, mouth wide. But the fangs closed only on feathers. The tail swung then like a great club, battering the bird. Prodromolu reeled and jerked at the blow but did not lose altitude. Three times the serpent attempted to catch him in a coil and three times failed. Again, the head came up and back, but Prodromolu parried the strike with his beak and strove for a greater altitude.

They mounted higher into the streak-shot air. The land was nearer now, and Talkne's weight hung limp and heavy in the dark bird's claws. The wing-beat tempo increased and a steady wind fanned the snake.

"Out of the water," Prodromolu said, "you are nothing but a stuffed skin, a sausage."

Talkne did not reply.

"I am Opener of the Way," he said after a time. "I go to throw wide the Gate, to bring the breath of fresh life."

"You will not depart this world," Talkne hissed.

Prodromolu swept on toward the land, its music and incense now reaching him across the water, a crowd of its orange-robed inhabitants waiting near the shoreline to be slain, singing and swaying as his shadow drew near. He opened his beak again and cried out to them.

As he approached the land he chose the spot with care, fled across the lower terraces and opened his claws as he banked and commenced a wide circle.

The serpent body writhed, twisting as it descended upon the city. Where it struck, buildings collapsed and people and demons were crushed, fountains were broken and fires sprang forth from the rubble. Prodromolu's head dropped and his wings swept back. He plunged toward his fallen adversary.

As he struck with his talons, Talkne's still body suddenly responded like a broken spring. A coil fell across his back and tightened immediately. Offbalanced, one wing pinned, feathers flying, Prodromolu was wrenched to one side and then over, and over again. More of the buildings collapsed, statues toppled, as they turned, rolled, fell. They descended the terraces, the ground shaking beneath them. The singing grew louder as they dropped toward the lowest level.

As the constriction of Talkne's body increased, Prodromolu tightened his own grip upon it and continued to strike and tear with his beak. Their blood mingled and spread in a series of coin-like pools. Orange-clad bodies lay all about them as the bird continued to hammer at the scaly form which imprisoned him in massive bands. At last there came a slight loosening of the serpent's coils, and the bird struck with renewed energy, tearing out chunks of flesh and dashing them aside into a small ornamental garden of silver-leafed shrubs.

He felt the serpent go limp. Dragging himself free, he struck once again, then threw back his head and uttered a piercing shriek. Then he spread his wings slowly, painfully, and lifted himself into the air.

The head of the serpent flashed upward and the mouth snapped shut upon his right leg. With a whiplike movement, Talkne cast

Prodromolu through the air and into the water, not letting go the leg, slithering immediately after to wind about the dark bird again.

"You will not depart this world," Talkne repeated, driving them out into deeper water.

"Pol!" said the other, suddenly. "You don't know what you're doing . . ."

There was a long pause, as the serpent dragged him even farther away from the shore. Then, "I know," came the reply.

Talkne dove, bearing Prodromolu along with him.

The bird tore partway free for an instant and drove his beak down upon the back of the serpent's head a bare instant before the fangs found the side of his neck and closed there.

As the waters roiled about him and the blow from that great beak fell upon the head of the serpent, Pol felt his consciousness fading and then everything seemed distant. Even as he locked his fangs more tightly upon the other, he felt insulated from the event, as if it really involved two other parties . . .

Thrashing frantically, he could not free himself from the grip upon his neck. As he was drawn ever more deeply beneath the water, Henry Spier felt the blackness rising and covering him over. He wanted to cry out. He reached to summon his powers, but he was gone before the necessary movement of Art could be completed.

XX.

He was walking. The mists were rolling all about him and the figures came and went. There was one very familiar one, with a message . . .

It was cold, very cold. He wanted a blanket, but something else was thrust into his hands. A warmth seemed to flow from it, however, and that was good. The moaning sounds ceased. He had barely been aware of them until then. He clutched more tightly at the object he held and something of strength came into him from it.

"Pol! Come on! Wake up! Hurry!"

The message . . .

He was aware that his face was being slapped. Face? Yes, he had a face.

"Wake up!"

"No," he said, his grip continuing to tighten upon the staff.

Staff?

He opened his eyes. The face before him was out of focus, but there was something familiar about it even then. It moved nearer to his own and the blurring vanished from its features.

"Mouseglove . . ."

"Get up! Hurry!" the small man enjoined him. "The others are stirring!"

"Others? I don't . . . Oh!"

Pol struggled to sit up and Mouseglove assisted him. As he did so, he saw that it was his father's scepter which he held clutched in his hands.

"How did you come by this?" he asked.

"Later! Take it and use it!"

Pol looked about the chamber. Larick had rolled onto his side, facing him. His eyes were open, though his expression was not one of comprehension. Across the chamber, near the door, Ryle Merson was moaning and beginning to move. From the corner of his eye, Pol saw that Taisa's arm was rising. He remembered Spier's words concerning a lapse of will, and he stared at the man, just as Spier began to sit up.

"Are they all enemies?" Mouseglove asked. "You'd better do something to the ones who are—fast!"

"Get out of here," Pol said. "Hurry!"

"I'll not leave you now."

"You must! However you came in—"

"Through the window."

"Back out it then. Go!"

Pol got up onto one knee and raised the scepter before him, staring at Henry Spier across it. Mouseglove moved out of sight, but Pol could not tell whether he had fled or only retreated. From somewhere, the smell of dragons came to his nostrils.

His arm was already throbbing, and he gave a grateful shudder that the power had not again deserted him. The statuette still stood in position upon the diagram, facing the Gate. He rose to his feet and sent his will into the scepter. There was an answering tingle in the palms of his hands. A sensation as of a protracted, subauditory organ note passed through him.

He felt no doubt whatsoever that Spier must die. If he let him live, he decided that he would be guilty of a greater offense than if he killed him, becoming himself responsible for any evil the man would work.

With a sound like a thunderclap, a sheet of almost liquid flame leapt from the scepter's tip to fall upon Henry Spier. The chamber was brilliantly illuminated and shadows ran relay races about the uneven walls.

Then the flame parted like a forked tongue, to reveal Spier standing beyond the bifurcation, right arm upraised.

"How'd you manage to get your hands on that thing?" he said, above the fire's roar.

Pol did not reply but bent all of his efforts to closing the fiery gap. Like a bloody pair of scissors in a shaky hand, it commenced swaying toward, then away from, the man in its midst. Pol felt the counterpressure growing and then waning, as Spier mustered his forces with occasional lapses.

"Your dragon outside the window, eh?" Spier said. "Must have him well-trained. Can't stand dragons myself. Smell like stale beer and rotten eggs."

The flames suddenly flew wide apart, like a letter Y, then a T. They began retreating toward Pol, the arms of the T slowly curving back around in his direction.

Pol gritted his teeth, and the flames' progress toward him was halted. He was seized with the sickening realization that even with his powers augmented by the scepter, Spier seemed to hold the edge. And Spier's strength was continuing to grow as he recovered, whereas his own appeared to have reached its limit. The flames began to sway again, but they were edging closer toward him. He knew that it was too late to shift to a different mode of attack, and he knew also that it would not make any difference if he could.

"It is a powerful tool that you hold," Spier stated slowly, as if reading his mind. "But a tool, of course, is only as good as the man who uses it. You are young, and but recently come into your powers. You are not sufficient to the task you have set yourself." He took a step forward and the flames roared ominously. "But then, I doubt that any man in this world is."

"Shut up!" Pol cried, and he tried to banish the flames, but they remained.

Spier took another step and halted as a surge of effort accompanying Pol's anger flicked them back a span in his direction.

"There can be only one outcome if you persist," Spier went on, "and I do not want that. Listen to me, boy. If you are good enough to give me as much trouble as you have, you are very good. I would regret very much having to destroy you, especially when there is no reason for it."

There came a loud report from the direction of the window, and a bullet ricocheted about the chamber. Spier glanced in that direction at the same time Pol did.

Mouseglove, standing outside, had rested his elbows upon the wide, stony sill. The pistol, pointed toward Spier, still smoked in his hand. He seemed to stiffen, and he slid away out of sight, the weapon clattering against stone as it fell.

Pol turned back in time to see Spier completing an almost casual gesture.

"Had I a moment or so more, I would have made him turn it against himself," he said. "But I can do that afterwards. Firearms are such a barbaric intrusion in this idyllic place, don't you think? I approve of your actions at Anvil Mountain, by the way. The Balance must be tipped toward more magic, where we will be supreme."

Panting now, Pol fended off the return of the flames, his dragonmark feeling as if it were itself afire. He knew that without the scepter he would be dead in the face of the present onslaught.

Spier seemed to be increasing even in stature now, as he recovered, an aura of poise and command growing about him.

"As I said, there is no reason for this," Spier continued. "I am willing to forgive our archetypal struggle beyond the Gate and what passed between us here before then. I feel that you still do not understand. I am also more convinced than ever of your suitability as an ally." He took a step backward and the pressure diminished. "A sign of my good faith," he said. "I have made the first move toward our easing away from this in stages. Let us call a halt and work together to our mutual benefit. I'll even teach you some unusual things about that staff you hold. I—"

Pol screamed and fell to his knees as his entire left side was seized and twisted by a hideous series of spasms. He thought that he felt his lower ribs give way.

Summoning all of his remaining energy, he drove it toward Spier in a gigantic psychic wedge, powered by fear, hate, a sense of betrayal, shame at his own gullibility . . .

"It wasn't me!" Spier cried—half in anger, half in surprise—as he was driven, tripping, back against the wall.

"Larick! Stop it . . ." came a weak voice from off to the right, as Ryle Merson struggled to his feet.

Instantly, the seizure halted, though its aftereffects left Pol kneeling, aching, shaking.

"Help him! Damn you!" Ryle cried, advancing. "That's Spier he's got against the wall!"

The fat man suddenly moved quickly and placed his hand upon the scepter below Pol's own. Immediately, Pol felt a partial easing of the tension which had held him for so long.

Spier's eyes, which had been wide, suddenly narrowed. Larick came up beside Pol on the left, his hand, also, coming to rest upon the scepter.

"You say I would use you," Spier said, "and this is true. But they are also guilty—of the same thing."

Pol bore down with his will, augmented by the others'. The flame leaped forward again—and halted, as if it had met an invisible wall.

He strove to increase his efforts and felt the others doing likewise, yet the situation remained unchanged. In fact, Spier was smiling—a small, almost sad smile.

"What's happening?" Pol said in a hoarse whisper.

"He's holding us," Ryle replied.

"All three of us?" Pol asked. "I almost had him myself before!"

"My little serpent," Spier said from across the chamber. "Although you surprised me several times, I was but testing your strength and letting things run long enough to give me the opportunity to speak with you. I see now that I have failed, and I must conclude things, though it really does my heart sore to see you put to waste. Good-bye—until some more agreeable life, perhaps."

He began to walk toward them. Immediately, the scepter became burning hot in Pol's grip. He clung to it despite this, however, and directed all of their energies toward halting the man, who now seemed the embodiment of strength and assurance. He felt some resistance, but Spier did not stop, and the smell of burning flesh came to his nostrils. His head swam, and for an instant the mists seemed to roil about him and the figure to his right was no longer Ryle Merson. What was he saying?

Spier doubled forward as if experiencing a sudden stomach cramp. He waved both his hands in small circles, frantically, the right before him, the left far out to the side.

After a moment, he straightened, the hand movements continuing but becoming more regular now, the circles growing. He looked ahead and then to the left.

"They're coming out of the woodwork now," he said ruefully.

Pol, who could no longer tell whether the scepter was hot, cold or lukewarm, turned his head toward the chamber's entrance.

Ibal and Vonnie stood there. He bore a white wand. She held what appeared to be a brass hand mirror, crosswise and close to her breast.

"You've roused the bloody geriatrics ward," Spier added, glaring now and appearing fully recovered. "We'll just have to retire them again."

His left hand changed its pattern, altered its rhythm. The metal mirror flashed as Vonnie swayed. Ibal laid a hand upon her shoulder and displayed his wand like an orchestra conductor at the opening of Brahms' Second Symphony.

"There *was* a time when you were good, old man," Spier said. "But you should have stayed retired . . ."

He flicked his right hand suddenly and Ryle Merson cried out and fell.

"A little misdirection never hurts," he said. "And then there were four . . ."

© JUDY KING RIENIETS 81

But his face showed signs of strain, and the mirror flashed again.

"Damned witch!" he muttered, retreating a step.

A needle-fine line of white light fled from the tip of Ibal's wand and pierced Spier's right shoulder. Spier bellowed as the arm fell to his side and a wave of fire and force from the scepter swept over him.

Clothing smouldering, he gestured wildly and the scepter was torn from Pol's and Larick's grip, spinning across the room and striking Ibal about the chest and shoulders as it turned. The white wand dropped to the floor as the sorcerer fell, his face already twenty years older.

The mirror flashed again and Spier seemed to catch its light with his left hand, from whence it was reflected upon Pol and Larick.

Pol felt it as a blow and was momentarily blinded. Falling, he struck against Larick, who was not strong enough to hold him. Both of them went down as Spier, his arm dripping blood, hair and eyebrows singed, face bright red, cloak smoking, turned toward the woman. He was muttering—whether profanity or the beginning of a spell, she was not certain.

"My dear lady," Spier said, advancing upon her, swaying. "It is all over."

Distantly, Pol heard her reply: "In that case, behold yourself."

He heard Spier's scream and thought that she had finished him. But then, at an even greater distance, he heard the man's weak answer: "Good. But not good enough."

But Pol was already walking through the place of mists, the form of the man so like himself at his side, telling him something, something to remember, something important . . .

"Belphanior!" he said aloud, half-raising his head.

And then he slumped and the mists rolled over him.

XXI.

My world was torn apart and reassembled in an instant. Possibly I, too, was subjected to the same process. My existential yearnings were redefined and satisfied by that single gesture. The perturbations of my spirit subsided. Everything—for the first time in my existence—was made clear to me. I reveled in the moment.

"Belphanior!"

Belphanior. Yes, Belphanior. It fit so beautifully, like an exquisite garment tailored just for me. I turned before the mirrors of my spirit, admiring the cut and the material.

I had been hurriedly assembled from the raw stuff of creation in this world by the sorcerer Det Morson on the day of his death— almost within minutes of it, actually. So rushed had he been by the unusually speedy advance of his enemies that he had been unable properly to conclude the work, to charge me in full with all of the necessary restrictions, compulsions and promptings. He rushed off to tend to his death without quite completing his spell and setting into motion all of those reflexes he had instilled. Or telling me who I was. Conscientious in the extreme, I realized, I had been trying to figure these matters out for myself.

It is very pleasing to learn of one's importance in the scheme of things.

And it is a good thing, in a very real sense, to have made one's own way in the world, unlike those others who came full-furnished with stocks of intellectual and emotional equipment suiting them for their comfortable niches in life and requiring never a second thought. Consider . . .

Det rushed off. I see now why he did not release me. Not only was I incomplete, without that final pronunciation of my name, but my infant strength would have been of small use against that army of besiegers and their wizard would doubtless have put me aside, likely rendering me useless for my true purposes. For how long after the fall of Rondoval I remained, trapped by the paraphernalia of the spell in that small chamber, I do not really know. Years, perhaps; until the natural erosions of time wore away the designs which barred my exit from that room. No true hardship, this; for my existence at that time was next to vegetable in character, not at all the inquiring and highly sophisticated state of mind I now enjoy. In the years which followed, I learned the geography of the place thoroughly, though I never questioned the nature of the force which kept me anchored to it—not even when I found that my modest forays into the countryside were invariably accompanied by an apprehension which was only allayed when I returned to the castle's confines. But I was young and naive. There were so many questions I did not yet ask. I slithered along rafters. I danced among moonbeams. Life was idyllic.

It was not until Pol's arrival and all of the activities which ensued that anything like a true curiosity was aroused in me. Beyond the vermin and some then incomprehensible dwellers upon other planes, my only experience with sentients had come from the minds of the sleeping dragons and their companions—hardly the most stimulating intellectual fare. But I was suddenly deluged with thoughts and words, and the ideas which lay behind them. It was then that I came into self-consciousness and first began to explore the enigmas of my own condition.

I know now that I was drawn to Pol because of his dragon-mark, and any of the horde of other cues which served to identify him to me at some primal level with my first accursèd master. I did not know, however, that this was a part of the design of my existence. In light of it, certain of my other actions became even more intelligible. Such as my animation of the corpse for purposes of conveying a message to Mouseglove. Such as my decision to depart Rondoval and follow Pol.

"Belphanior." Delicious word.

As Pol lay semiconscious, gasping, aching, suffering from a number of burns, broken bones, sprains, abrasions, contusions and near-total fatigue, I realized that an important part of my mission in life involved his protection and I was pleased to have succeeded as well as I had, considering the handicap under which I was working. It gratified me that I had occasionally relieved the pressure of some of his more distressing dreams, not to mention sending Mouseglove after the scepter, without which he would almost certainly by now have been dead.

Yes, it pleased me that I had done the right things when I had acted, had reached so many proper conclusions by virtue of my own initiative rather than because of any standing order I was obliged to follow. As I considered the fallen form of Larick—also under my protection—as well as those of Ryle, Ibal and the rapidly failing lady Vonnie, I was happy to know that by extension, as allies, I could also count them as being in my care. The philosophical vistas now opened to me seemed almost limitless.

Yes.

With the pronunciation of my name I was immediately aware of who and what I was:

I am the Curse of Rondoval (a technical term, that), existing to defend both the premises and the members of the House, and failing that, to avenge them.

I look upon it as a challenging, exciting and wonderful occupation.

It is with extreme gratitude that I now consider the fact that Det Morson, hard-pressed as he was there at the end, yet managed to find time for the creation of a good Curse.

As I watched Henry Spier and Vonnie swaying and staggering back and forth, hurling their remaining energies through intricate and deceptive patterns at one another in a conflict to determine the fate of my charges, not to mention that of the world, I realized that, despite the forces which had been thrown against him, the man had the edge and would doubtless in a few moments emerge victorious. It was instructive to follow his magical manipulations. There was genuine artistry there, as I understood it. The man had, after all, once been a peer and close friend of my accurséd master. It was, in this sense, unfortunate that he had become an enemy of Rondoval and, hence, the designated recipient of my wrath.

Which led me to another important train of considerations: With Det Morson dead these two decades and two heirs of Rondoval visible on the floor, who was his proper successor as my accurséd master? Larick was Pol's senior, yet he had forsaken the family precincts to dwell at Avinconet. Pol, on the other hand, maintained his residence at the family seat and thus was more sensitive to the needs of Rondoval itself. Witness, his ongoing program of repair and renovation. The matter could, over the years, become very important when it came to the assigning of priorities in my work-schedule.

I resolved it finally in Pol's favor. Possibly, ultimately, a sentimental choice. While I allowed myself to be swayed by the argument from residence, I was not unaware that my decision could easily have been colored by the fact that I knew Pol better than I did his brother and that I had not approved of Larick's earlier actions against him. Or, to put it more simply, I liked Pol better.

I drifted near his twitching, recumbent form, and for the first time attempted direct communication with him.

Everything is all right now, accurséd master, I reported, *except for a few details.*

He began coughing just as Vonnie screamed, interfering with his acknowledgement.

I regarded Henry Spier once more, his face twisted and blackened, as he tied the final knots of his spell. I noted, too, that Ryle Merson was awake and struggling to raise one arm. Larick and Ibal were likely to remain unconscious for some time longer. Taisa was sitting up and looking very bewildered.

I reviewed a number of possible actions I might take against Spier, rejecting many—even the one which involved flooding the chamber by diverting a nearby underground stream, a course which possessed a great esthetic appeal for me.

Finally, the choices were narrowed to one and the only remaining detail involved my decision as to the proper color scheme.

Avocado, ranging to a very pale green, I finally decided.

XXII.

When Pol heard the voice in his head, he rolled onto his side and opened his eyes. He lacked the strength to do anything more. The situation appeared virtually unchanged so far as he could tell. Vonnie seemed no longer a young woman, but middle-aged and tired-looking. Spier also looked worn, but there was still some vitality in his gestures. A moment more and it appeared that the man would win.

There came a loud hissing sound from the back of the chamber. Spier glanced in that direction and his face froze. His hands halted in mid-gesture. Vonnie also looked that way, with identical results.

Pol struggled to turn his head, and when he succeeded he beheld a particularly ghastly materialization. It appeared to be the demon body he himself had briefly worn, taking rapid shape beside the table—headless. In place of a head, it wore a crown of flames—avocado, ranging to a very pale green.

Pol heard Taisa shriek. And from their changing expressions, it appeared that Spier and Vonnie each thought the other responsible for the phenomenon.

In that moment, a bit of light fled from between Ryle Merson's cupped hands to fall upon Spier's breast. Spier staggered back, gesturing as if to brush it away and casting a quick glance in Ryle's direction.

Pol raised his hand and moved it as if engaged in a sorcerous manipulation, though the power was gone, the dragonmark still once again. Spier made a warding movement just as the voice boomed out:

"The Curse of Rondoval is upon you, Henry Spier!"

The flame-headed demon-form lurched forward, and Spier—all color fled from his face—turned and seized the statuette, which he raised before him.

"I have served you!" he cried. "Now it's your turn! Now, or never!"

© JUDY-BING RENIETS 81

There came a flash of light from Vonnie's mirror, directed toward Spier, simultaneous with a heavy scraping sound from the direction of the table.

The light from the mirror did not reach Spier. Somewhere in the vicinity of the figurine—at arm's length before him—it appeared to be absorbed. The jewels in the statuette suddenly shone like tiny, colored fires.

A dark shape rushed forward, racing the demon-form toward Spier. It passed the creature—a heavy wooden armchair from beside the table—passed Spier also, pivoted in midair, dropped and pushed forward, striking Spier behind the knees.

The sorcerer collapsed into the chair, still clutching the blazing icon.

The chair tilted backward and levitated rapidly, just as the Curse of Rondoval sprang toward it. It swung in a wide arc about the room and the fire-crowned avenger bounded after it.

It rushed at the wall, banked suddenly, then shot directly toward the window.

Belphanior recovered his balance, turned, and sprang after it, talons extended. He caught the edge of Spier's long yellow cloak which trailed behind.

The chair jerked and Spier made a gagging sound, clawing at his throat with one hand. Then its clasp tore loose and the cloak fell away. The chair resumed its forward motion, picking up speed, and passed out through the window.

Pol heard a startled cry followed by a dragon's roar. A moment later, there were gunshots. Then he heard Mouseglove cursing. He propped himself with one stiff arm and started to sway. He felt Ryle's hand upon his shoulder, steadying him.

"Easy . . ." Ryle said. "He's been checked. We're safe."

Ryle helped him into a sitting position, then looked toward Taisa, Larick, Vonnie.

The old woman was sitting upon the floor, the mirror at her side. She held Ibal's head in her lap and was speaking softly, almost crooning, above him. When she felt Ryle's gaze, she raised one hand to cover her face. Ryle quickly looked away.

Larick was stirring again. Ryle rose slowly, ponderously, to his feet and made his way toward his daughter. Pol caught only one brief glimpse of his face.

"Accurséd master," Belphanior said then, prostrating himself before him. "I have answered your summons. I apologize that the man escaped my wrath."

"What— Who are you?" Pol asked, moving his suddenly warm foot back from the bowed, avocado to pale green-flamed head. "And please rise."

"Belphanior, the Curse of Rondoval, your servant," he said, raising himself into a semi-erect stance.

"Really?"

"Yes. You called and I answered. I would have dismembered him for your delight, save for that unfair chair trick."

"Perhaps you'll have another opportunity one day," Pol said. "But thank you for this service. It was timely, and well done."

Belphanior handed him the yellow cloak.

"Your own garments are in need of repair. Perhaps the sorcerer's robe . . ."

"Thanks."

Pol took it into his hands. The light fabric felt strange, yet at the same time familiar. There was a small patch of white on the inside, below the collar. He raised it and looked more closely.

CUSTOM-MADE IN HONG KONG ran the words upon it.

He almost dropped the cloak as he was taken by a sudden chill.

"May I assist you, accursèd master?"

"No. I'll manage."

He drew it about his shoulders and fastened it at the neck. He straightened his legs painfully, rising upon them. The ache in his left side grew stronger. Larick, too, was attempting to rise. He extended his hand. Larick looked at it for a moment, then took it and pulled himself up. He did not release it for a moment, however, but continued to stare at the dragonmark. Then he looked up at Pol's hair.

"I never knew," he said at last.

"I only learned at the last possible moment myself," Pol said.

Over his shoulder, Pol saw that Mouseglove was seated upon the windowsill, staring. A moment later, the small man shouted something out the window and dropped to the floor.

"Moonbird couldn't follow the chair," he called out. "It was moving too fast."

Pol nodded. As Mouseglove came toward him, he saw that Ryle and Taisa were also approaching.

Larick turned toward the woman, smiling. She moved past him, placed her arms about Pol's neck and kissed him.

"Thank you," she said, at last. "I thought this day would never come, till wandering in spirit I saw you brought here. I knew somehow that you would free me."

As he gazed past her, Pol saw a peculiar look pass over Larick's face. He disentangled himself quickly, pushed her gently back and bowed despite his aching side.

"I am pleased to have helped," he said, "but it was hardly my doing alone. It was simply—circumstance."

"You are modest."

Pol turned away.

"We'd best see to Ibal and Vonnie immediately."

The old sorcerer looked young again but was still unconscious. Vonnie's beauty had for the most part returned and its enhancement continued as Pol watched. She smiled up at him.

"He'll be all right," she said. "I just wanted to keep him from awakening until the cosmetic spell was in place. We can repair the rejuvenation spells later."

She picked up the magic mirror and regarded herself in it. She smiled.

"Vanity, I know," she said. "Delightful thing."

"Let us," Ryle said, coming up beside them, "repair to more congenial quarters. Perhaps your servant can bring Ibal, Pol."

"That will not be necessary," Vonnie answered, holding the mirror before Ibal's face.

Ibal's eyes opened. He considered his reflection, then began to rise.

"Lead on," she said. "We will follow."

XXIII.

Night had fallen. In a large chamber in the castle Avinconet, six jeweled figurines were grouped at the center of a series of concentric circles painted upon the floor; among these circles and about them various Words and Signs had also been executed. It had taken the entire day to situate them so, for every possible thing that could have gone wrong—from spilled paint, mispronounced Words, incorrectly drawn figures, a series of earth tremors and troops of marauding vermin who had marred the pattern—had gone wrong.

At last, however, the final spell had been pronounced, the final line drawn, the final gesture executed. Immediately, the interference had ceased. The Keys were contained.

Now Pol, Larick, Ibal, Vonnie, Ryle, Taisa, Mouseglove and Belphanior sat, reclined, stood, paced, drifted as an invisible cloud, took refreshment, rested and conferred at the farther end of the large room.

". . . Then I don't understand why they didn't help Spier," Mouseglove was saying.

"I believe that they were helping Spier all along," Ryle replied, "but we finally exhausted them, too, for a little while. Long enough, though. Almost."

"You say that, theoretically, he could still open the Gate with the one Key?" Mouseglove asked.

"He told Pol that he could, and I believe that he's right. It would probably take a lot of effort, though. I just don't know for certain. He's the greatest living authority."

"What now?" Larick asked, from where he sat beside Taisa who was looking at Pol who was looking at the book he held in his lap.

"They're neutralized now, but I will not rest until all seven Keys are destroyed," Ryle said. "They could still be stolen or freed somehow and the thing could start all over again."

"I can guard them against mortal thieves for a time," Mouse-glove offered.

. . . And I against those of the other variety, Belphanior said from somewhere.

"But *can* they be destroyed?" Taisa asked. "After everything we tried on them earlier . . ."

"Everything that exists has some weakness," Ibal said, lowering his goblet. "We will have to explore carefully."

"It's in here," Pol said. "Far back, and scattered, but our father did leave some clues. I've already come across a few new ones. I am going to have to read through the entire thing now and put them all together. It will take a while . . ."

"It must be done," Larick said.

"Yes."

"I cannot help but admire their vision," Ibal said. "You know, if I were Madwand rather than a traditionally trained man of the Art, I don't believe that I would be sitting here with you."

Ryle looked at him sharply.

Ibal chuckled.

"Don't give me that look," he said. "You were in on it at the beginning, till you learned that one important fact. And if you had been Madwand, what then, Ryle?"

Ryle looked away.

"I can't deny it," he said. "It's wrong, but I hate them as much for shattering that vision as for anything else."

"I did not say it just to irritate you," Ibal continued, "but as a caution: Trust no more Madwands than those here present—unless they be well-proven."

"You think Spier may now seek allies?"

"Wouldn't you?"

"I believe I am onto something," Pol said, turning a page. "I don't think this is going to be easy . . ."

A feeling of tension came into the room, as if the air pressure had suddenly been raised. It built for several seconds and then subsided.

"What was that?" Mouseglove asked.

The Keys attempted to shatter their confines, Belphanior announced. *But they failed. Your spells proved more than adequate.*

"Very promising," Larick said. "Keep reading, brother. And mark that passage."

Later, invisible and drifting, I was the only audience save for a drowsing dragon, when Pol sat upon the ramparts of Avinconet and played his guitar, slowly, with bandaged hands. I counted myself fortunate to have gained my name and found my calling in life that day. As I listened to his song, I decided that he must not be too bad, as accurséd masters go. I rather liked his music.

Then a strange thing happened, for my perceptions are not as their perceptions and I like to feel that they are far less readily tricked. The moon broke forth from behind a cloud, infusing the land with its pale light; and falling upon him there, it made it seem for a moment that Pol's hair was white with a dark streak down the middle, rather than the other way around. In that moment, I recalled an infant perception of my creator, and it seemed that I looked again upon the face of Det overlaying Pol's own, masklike. The image had a more than natural strength in the impression it made upon me, and the memory it created was somehow an uncomfortable thing.

But it was gone in an instant, and the music continued. Is life a quick illusion or a long song? I asked myself, as I was in need of new philosophical pursuits.

© JUDY KING RIENIETS 81

QUALITY PRINTING AND BINDING BY:
ORANGE GRAPHICS
P.O. BOX 791
ORANGE, VA 22960 U.S.A.